MOON CHASED

THE GREAT TEAR DUET
BOOK I

JOEY KINCAID

Cover Design by: Nicole Kincaid

POV Art by: Joey Kincaid

Editing by: Nicole Kincaid

First Paperback Edition: June 2024

DEDICATION

For my wife, who struggled for years and continues to fight through. Your strength inspires me to persevere even when I can't see the light.

For those that linger in the darkness, unable to see through it for the glimmer of hope. Within you burns a light that no pain or hardship could extinguish.

ACKNOWLEDGMENTS

The first person I want to thank is my wife, Nicole. Without your support I would never have been able to finish this book. If I am being honest, without you this probably would have been one of the hundreds of projects I have started only to stop the next day. You have always stood by me, never making me feel bad for wanting to try new things. You were the first person to read my writing when I felt self-conscious, cheering me on and making me feel like a million bucks. I love you so much. Thank you for being my light when I'm in the dark.

To my Alpha Readers, Nicole Kincaid and David Dietz. You took precious time away from your passions and your families to read through the roughest version of my work. It means the world to me that you took that time to give me feedback and make my work the best it could be. Thank you.

Thank you to Andi Eloise @andieloisevoice and Branden Davis-Butler @brandenisagirlnametoo for narrating lines from my book during the 2023 #HumanVoicesOnly campaign. Your wonderful skills in bringing words to life had me in tears and feeling like I was watching one of my children walk for the first time. Thank you.

To my amazing Beta Readers!

Lynsey Martini, @bookish.and.ballet, you were the very first person from outside my immediate circle to finish the book front to back! I was so terrified when I sent out my beta copies of the book and received your kind words when I had felt my lowest. You truly gave me the encouragement to stick with it. From the bottom of my heart, thank you so much for giving me a chance. It was a complete honor to have you on my team!

Grace Derr, when I started the journey with social media and self promoting I had no idea what I was doing, and let me be honest, I still don't. But you were a shining light of positivity. When I sent out requests for Beta Readers and got your submission it was a no brainer on whether I would send you a copy. Then when you sent me updates as you were reading, I practically screamed with excitement at the fact that you were enjoying it. I hope that you are surrounded by just as much love and positivity as your shine on others! Thank you so very much for being on my team and helping push me forward on this incredible journey!

To all of my ARC Readers, you are the backbone of a successful book release. You are the trailblazers of the reading community. Pushing through and reading books that others wouldn't even give a chance without your honest rating or reviews. You could be reading any book right now, so whether you enjoy my story or not, I want to thank you for giving me the chance to share this with you.

CONTENT WARNING

This book contains very difficult situations that may be troubling to some readers. These situation include, substance abuse, graphic violence, death, murder, kidnapping, torture, imprisonment, sexually explicit material, sexual assault, mental illness, references to current or past suicidal thoughts and actions.

Suicide can touch anyone, anywhere, and at any time. But it is not inevitable. There is hope.

If you are feeling alone and having thoughts of suicide—whether or not you are in crisis—or know someone who is, don't remain silent. Talk to someone you can trust through the 988 Suicide & Squad Crisis Lifeline. Call or text 988 or chat the lifeline.

Your mental health matters. You matter.

CHAPTER 1

I've always felt safest in the forest, far from the watchful eyes of the village.

The leaves crunch beneath my worn leather boots as I walk through the dense redwood forest that surrounds the village. Warmth fills my chest despite the chilled breeze brushing against my fur lined leathers. I appreciate the vibrant orange and yellow leaves clinging to life on the branches around me. Rubbing my bare hands together and blowing out a slow breath between them. *At least the snow hasn't begun to fall.*

While most of the plants are wilting due to the sudden chill, the nitter berries should be ripe for picking. I look down at the pint-sized clay jar on my belt. Altha's raspy voice playing in my mind, *"I expect it to be full this time Alex. The harvesting window is closing and we will need that jar come spring."*

She was right to be upset, the last time I had come out I had completely forgotten to gather even one berry. Instead, I got lost in the wondrous sounds and smells of the forest.

I close my eyes, taking a slow, deep breath in through my nose. The scent of the leaves that had just crunched beneath my feet hit me first. The fresh steam rising from where the sun's rays had finally reached. I push those to the side, taking in another steady breath. *There it is.* The familiar stale and earthy scent fills my nose as I open my eyes and turn directly for it.

Altha often told me that it was remarkable how I could list off the ingredients in any one of her brews just by smelling it. I had never told her that I could also smell them half a mile away from her hut. Or that I could tell her what George, the self-proclaimed Lord of Red River, had eaten for dinner the night before. I had learned the hard way that it wasn't normal to follow smells like a dog looking for freshly baked butter bread.

The smell of the nitter berries grows stronger after a few minutes of walking. "Found you," I whisper. The large bush with thorn covered leaves coming into view just on the other side of a shallow creek. The rocks shimmer just beneath the water's surface. I kneel near the edge, my sky-blue eyes reflecting off the water's surface, the cold sting of the water against my bony fingers as I take a shallow sip. Drying them through my honey hair, strands of gold glinting in the sun.

I gently close my eyes, letting my breath steady as I take in the sounds around me. Listening doesn't come as easy to me as smells. But if I focus... The cracking of the branches came from above first, the soft padded feet of a squirrel landing on another branch, the huff of a deer before it digs into its breakfast.

No wolves... I rise to my feet and gingerly approach the bush. I carefully push the leaves aside, without pricking my fingers, revealing the deep red berries that smell of stale earth. I fill the jar that Altha had given me, placing it into my satchel with care.

A branch tugs at my shoulder, the concerning tug followed by the familiar sound of tearing leather.

I sigh, my fingers running along the open seam. I haven't been able to scrape together the coin for new clothes since I was twelve. It's much cheaper to just mend what I have by adding length when and where I need it. Assuming I could afford the needed leather, of course.

Altha does wondrous work for the village as their Apothecary. Setting broken bones, brewing remedies for the sick, even guiding the mothers through birth. Yet she never took even a single coin for her efforts. When I was old enough to ask her why she only looked at me with that one raised eyebrow, her wrinkled skin following it and said, *"Health and wellbeing is a right not a privilege Alex."*

The leaves in the trees above me shake as a rush of wind blows past me, the fresh smell of clean air filling my lungs. *It's going to rain soon.* I had best get back to Altha's hut, or risk sitting next to the fire trying to dry off while she scolded me for getting caught in the rain.

I step onto the grass, leaving the forest behind as the crisp, sunset breeze carries the familiar scent of earth and iron that always fills Altha's hut. It sits at the base of a hill with a thatched roof in dire need of replacement. The earth curving up the wooden walls as if desperately trying to reclaim what was taken from it.

Home... for what it is. I have always felt more at home in the forest. At least until the sun began to set, the vast darkness creeping around every tree as my stomach tightens.

I force a grin to my face, my cheeks reminding me of how hard it is to wear the mask of happiness. She cares for me though, and I need to ensure she thinks everything is ok.

"Hey Altha, I'm back!" I shout, stepping through the front door.

Altha looks up at me, the faint gray of her hair hanging down over the shoulders of her brown gown. She leans heavily on her twisting wooden cane that ends in a large knot. "*Hmm...* It's about time, did you at least get the berries this time?"

I merely pull the jar out forcing my grin to go up a little more as the smell of the iron begins to give me a headache.

"Did someone get hurt?" I ask, looking at the large table in the back of the room that we never eat at. I have seen too many injured people lay upon that table while Altha twisted, pulled or threaded wounds... the sounds they would make often had me running for anywhere that wasn't here.

"Oooh, yes... Michael had an axe head break clean off. It spun back and lodged into his shoulder. Told him that if he spent half as much time tending his tools as he does chasing Emily he wouldn't have been on my table today," she mussed, pointing over to the pot already boiling on the fire. "Grind up the berries and add them to the pot, the redwood bark is already in."

I do as she says, grinding the berries with the mortar and pestle she had out next to the pot with patient hands. The grin on my face no longer fake due to the thought of Mike walking his way here in pain. He had become the strongest, if not the dumbest woodcutter in generations.

"Are you sure this will be enough to last through Spring?" I ask, Altha now shifting back and forth in her cherished white oak rocking chair, a soft quilt over her lap.

"Well, I suppose that is up to you, isn't it," she scolds, not so much a question as she looks down her nose at me. "If you would stop taking the Nitpaw at the first chance and instead practice your breathing like I taught you, it would last a lot longer."

"It's not my fault, the attacks... they have been hitting a lot harder this last year."

"That's because you rely too much on the Nitpaw!" Altha's brow furrows, waving her hand halfheartedly at me. "Finish adding the berries so they can simmer overnight."

Discussing my attacks always ends like that, me defending myself and Altha just brushing it off like I'm still a child. When I was little I would have maybe one attack a week, usually only at night. Now... they come so frequently that it feels as though the very ground beneath my feet wants to swallow me whole.

I work in silence for nearly an hour. Scraping the last bit into the pot, I look up at Altha. She looks so peaceful, the faint moonlight trickling in through the only window in the hut. She often falls asleep here, watching out that window as if at any time someone is going to come barreling down the hill from the village in need of her help.

I pull the quilt up a little more, letting my fake smile fall away as I tuck her in. My cheeks feel sore from the effort, but I know that it brings her some comfort in believing everything is ok. I stoke the fire with a few more logs before making my way to my room.

It isn't much, but Altha did what she could when my mom left. Converting a portion of this small storage closet into my own personal space. There isn't a door, but I am happy for it. No door means that the cauldron's fire can battle away the ever vigilant shadows that try to grab at my feet.

There is just enough room for my bag at the foot of my hay bed. The narrow slats along the roof let wisps of light come through that keep the shadows at bay without me having to worry over a window. I remove my leathers, unlacing them down one side to make a quick blanket, noting the torn shoulder that I still need to get a cord for soon. My tattered under shirt and pants are just enough to protect against the chilly night air. I lay down, focusing on the gentle breeze that whispers through the slats, letting it carry me to sleep. To the forests of my dreams.

The crisp morning mist tickles my nose as the sun leaks in through the slats along the roof. I throw my leathers back on and meet Altha in the main room. "Good morning," I said, my fake smile already in place.

"Good morning," she said, putting the stopper in a fresh vial of Nitpaw. "When you're done with breakfast, I need you to make a run to George's place."

"Oh... well I was gonna..."

"Go to George's... Then you can come right back and practice your remedies," Altha snapped with a finger pointed at me.

I grunt, tearing a chunk off the jerky I had grabbed from my cupboard stash. "What do you even need from George's anyway? We just got rations two nights ago."

"Don't you get that tone with me, boy. Paula came by and told me Sarfu arrived in the village last night. I have a letter for him to take and am expecting something to have arrived as well." Altha's nose crinkles as she continues filling vials.

Sarfu's Caravan makes an appearance every few months regardless of the weather but rarely stays for more than a day before moving on. While most people in the village look down on non-humans, especially magical beings, they always were respectful to Sarfu. Probably because without him Red River, our village, would not be able to communicate or trade with the outside world.

"Did Paula happen to say if Emily would be there today?" I ask.

"She didn't," she said, her face tightening with frustration.

"I overheard some of the villagers whispering about hearing screams coming from the Mills' house in the dead of night. Some even mentioned seeing flashes of light coming from their windows."

"Don't you go trusting a lick of that. Gossip is as good as mud water, till you filter out all the filth you don't have anything worth sharing," she rasped, waving a ladle in my direction. "I best not hear of you whispering falsehoods, all it does is hurt folk."

"Who would I tell?" I ask, walking to the stump of a chair. Snatching the letter and handful of Nitpaw vials Altha had left there. "Alright…" I huffed out, resigned to the fact that I am not getting out of going to the village today. "See you tonight."

"This afternoon Alex!"

The cloud cover doesn't do much to warm my spirits as I crest the hill that separates Altha's hut from Red River. I feel the cold sting of the wind against my cheeks, my nose filling with the fresh scent of redwood shavings as I look to the massive mill and trade house. They were the first two buildings that George's family built when they settled here. Since then, several houses have popped up around them, all made from the very lumber they ship out to our Elven Lords.

The Nitpaw coats my mouth in a bitter film as I drop the now empty vial back into the satchel before making my way into the village. I hurry past the houses and right up to George's trade house, noting the caravan carts parked just across the way.

I hear Sarfu's booming voice before reaching the door, "Don't you be trying to pull the wool over my eyes George Mills!"

"I would never... we just haven't had a good enough season to be parting with that much lumber for such a small sum," George replied just as I stepped inside.

The stench of ale and vomit permeates every inch of the polished wood. George's scruffy red beard, the only hair on his head, helps to elongate his round face. Today he is wearing a brand new brown leather vest that looks strange over his thick wool sweater.

"Alex! Welcome in, pull up a chair and I'll be right with you," George says.

Across the counter from George stands Sarfu. Nearly a foot taller than George, Sarfu practically has to hunch his shoulders to not hit the ceiling. Which only unnecessarily emphasizes each of his muscles. A two-headed axe, nearly as tall as him, rests against the counter beside him. No one has seen him wield the weapon but it always seems to gleam at the slightest fleck of light that comes near it.

"Thank you for the offer Mr. Mills, but Altha just wanted for me to hand off a letter to Sarfu while he was in town. She also mentioned you might have something for her?" I ask, holding the envelope out to Sarfu.

"Yes, yes... let me get it out of my bag," Sarfu says just before throwing back his mug, draining its contents with a sigh before snatching the letter and reaching over to his large multi-pocketed bag. "Aahhhh, here it is."

I snatch the small envelope from his hands, quickly sliding it into my satchel and turning for the door. I come up short as a slender girl's arms shoot around me, squeezing tight.

"I knew Sarfu coming around would bring you out of that forest," Emily squeaked. She is definitely the fairest of the girls in Red River. Her golden curls flow down to just beneath her narrow shoulders.

"Hello to you too Emily," I say, gently pushing her forward. The faint smell of stale pine drifts across my nose telling me that the white and blue gown she is wearing is new. Having not yet been smothered by the overwhelming scent of roses that always seems to follow her around.

She smoothly floats around me while loosening her hold before hooking her arm around mine. "Would you mind walking me to Paula's?" The squeeze of her hand, a silent plea.

I glance at her father. His brow furrowed as his eyes shoot daggers at our entwined arms. "You have chores that need doing," George grumbled.

Emily's shoulders tighten, her head falling to the floor. "Please daddy? I haven't been out of the house since..."

"Do I not provide enough?" George cut her off, ale splashing out of his mug as he brought it down on the counter with a *thud*. "All I ask is for a little respect!"

Time slows, the walls closing in around me, my eyes sliding between George and his daughter, her nails digging into my hand. I can hear my blood pumping harder and harder, the muscles in my legs screaming at me to run.

"Now, now George," Sarfu slowly growled. "Let the girl have some gossip time with her aunt. We have much to discuss as it is." I could hear the wood of his mug groan as his eyes locked with George's.

George's face tightens in on itself even further, his knuckles as white as marble. His eyes dart to mine. Burning through me as he throws back his mug, ale dripping down his chin as he said, "Fine... but you best be home to make dinner before sundown."

Without waiting for Emily's response, I shuffle us out the door. Flinching as the door slams shut behind us. I gasp for air, pulling out a vial of Nitpaw with one hand and popping the cork with my thumb as I throw it back.

The bitter liquid works fast. My vision sharpens as my lungs finally fill with air. The sound of my heart finally slowing to a normal rhythm.

Emily's sad eyes watch me as she grips my shoulder. "I'll be fine," I said, shoving the empty vial in my bag.

We walk for a short distance in silence, her home finally disappearing behind a few houses as she spins around burying her face in my chest. I slowly wrap my arms around her, frozen by her muffled sobs against my stitched leathers.

A chill runs down my spine as I hold her in my arms, terrified she might crumble away. Gently, I guide us over to the nearby bench, the warm glow of the brazier beside it offering little reprieve from the chill in my bones.

She rests against me until her tears subside, drying her face with her sleeves before looking into my eyes. *What should I say? I couldn't... no... wouldn't, do anything... I had done nothing...*

"Thank you," she said, her head gently resting on my shoulder again.

For what? I had been worthless, Sarfu had created the opening for us to escape... I had just... stood there.

"I think I understand now... why you hide in the forest. You feel him there don't you, your Da?"

Any chance that the fire had to break the chill inside me snuffed out at those words. "I..."

"I feel my mom all over the house. I feel her hand brush my cheek as I wake... the sound of her scrubbing the dishes after supper beside me." Tears begin to well in her eyes, her arm tightening around mine. "She's gone." Her voice cracks, her tears flowing in full force once more.

The air feels impossibly cold now, as if the brazier beside us had been snuffed out by her tears. *What do I do, what do I say?* Each beat of my heart aches, the pain leaching throughout my entire body.

"She loved you," I whisper, my jaw tight with each word.

"I miss her," she says between sobs.

The smell of roses and ale still cling to my nose as I approach the edge of the village. With Emily safe in her Aunt

Paula's house, a slight warmth fills my chest. Remembering how she had thanked me. That I had somehow helped.

That warmth vanished as fast as it had come as Todd and Ben step out from around the corner, large axes hanging limply at their sides. Neither one of them were tall but they were both covered in muscle gained from their work as woodcutters.

I slowed to a stop, looking from side to side.

"*Tsk tsk tsk*. Alex, I thought we had an understanding, you and I." Mike said from behind me. His shoulder, still wrapped in Altha's bandages from the day before. His short brown hair spiked forward, mirroring his pointed jaw.

"Hey Mike... w-what do you mean?" I ask, feeling my chest tighten. My hands move to my chest, gripping the straps of my bag.

"Come on now, you know I hate repeating myself," Mike said, snapping his fingers. Todd and Mike grip my arms, holding me in place. Mike grinning as he twists a club in one hand, his heavily muscled arm flexing with the slow rotation.

My throat feels tight, my eyes threatening to pop from my head as I look between the three men, "I-I'm not... what..."

"Emily!" Mike roars, pushing his nose against mine. "You know perfectly well that she is mine," Mike says, his eyes wide with rage.

Sweat builds in my palms, shadows creeping in around me, trapping me here with them, *with him*. "L-look... Mike... I... nothing happened..." I pushed out, my breathing becoming more rapid.

"Don't you lie to me. I saw you with her on that bench," he said, thrusting the club toward the bench across the way.

My eyes widen, my face flushing of heat. "Mike I... I swear... I was just taking her to..."

"I said don't you lie to me!" Mike roars, driving the top of the club into my gut.

My legs buckle, unable to hold me as I gasp for air. Todd and Ben release their hold, sending me crashing to my knees. My arms wrap around my stomach, each breath exploding from my lungs in a cough. The shadows around me threaten to swallow everything I am as I look up.

Todd and Ben chuckle above me, just as the first boot slams into my chest. I throw my arms in front of my face desperate to hold off any of the blows, "Stop! Please!" I scream between kicks, pain jolting through me with each impact. I twist to one side, hearing a boot slam against the ground. I roll again, only to receive a boot to the face followed by an audible *crunch*.

I can barely hear anything other than my heartbeat, my vision barely a spec of the world I once knew. Mike fists my hair, pulling me to my knees, "Don't you ever come back here," he said. The *crack* of the club shattered the last bit of light, plunging everything into darkness.

CHAPTER 2

The smell of burning redwood and earth fills my nose as I crack open my swollen eyes. My bones feel like glass as I push them under me. Every muscle screams in agony before finally giving out, slamming my face back into the ground.

"Altha... how lon..." my throat tightens like a vice, sending me into a coughing frenzy.

"Hey now, I didn't work this hard for you to up and die on me now. Here, drink this," a large male figure said, placing a waterskin against my lips.

The ice-cold, smooth liquid floods down my desert-like throat as I gulp it down.

"Woah, woah now. If you drink it like that, it's gonna come right back up," the man said, pulling the waterskin away. I can't quite place the voice as I look up at him. He is a blur, a *giant* blur. "Slow and steady, take a bite of this and then you can drink some more."

I take a deep breath in through my nose, the food he is holding out smells like mold that mixes with the alcohol floating up from his sleeve. I swallow back the bile building in my throat, my palm pressing against my lips.

"See? I told you. You have been out for three days, I bet Mindi here that you wouldn't make it," the man says, gesturing to another blurry figure across the fire. He grips one of my hands, placing the food into my palm. "Guess I owe you that meat, huh girl?"

It feels creamy, yet solid as my teeth sink into the yellow ball. "Where am I? Who are you?"

"Oh, where are my manners? I am Sarfu. Here, I am going to help you see a bit better."

I quickly pull back, my back pressing against an old log that creaks under my weight.

"Now hold on. If I wanted to hurt you, I would have just dumped you when I found you hidden in my cart." He put something up just above my eyes. The cold metal sending shivers down my spine as he firmly cups the back of my head with his other hand.

I can hear the blood pumping in my ears. He applies gentle pressure and then within a blink of an eye, he has a rag in place of the cold iron, pressing one of my hands against it. "There see, barely any pain. I guess with swelling like that you probably have plenty of other pain though," he said, chuckling to himself as he walked back around the fire.

I enjoy a few moments of quiet, the crackling fire coming into focus as I polish off the yellow ball of food. Washing it down with the frigid water.

Before long the bleeding stops and I am looking around. The moonlight and stars cast a warm glow over the miles of grass and hills in every direction, not a single redwood in sight. I look back at Sarfu, finding him perched against a log, one hand holding a shiny red apple. The other, petting the gray fur of a hound that, even laying down, is just under his shoulders. Its entire body is riddled with muscles layered over one another. "What... where are we?"

"About half a day away from my next stop, four days out from Red River."

"What?" I shout, my eyes pinching together. "Why didn't you take me back after you found me?"

"Honestly? I wasn't sure you would make it through the night, let alone these last few days. Plus the frost is already coming this way so I don't have the supplies or time to lose getting you back there right now. Besides, you have to cover the cost of me keeping you alive," he said, pitching another log on the fire.

"I'm grateful for you helping me but..."

"Helping?" Sarfu grunts, glancing sideways at me.

The hound didn't move but its green eyes were watching me now. *Was it even asleep before?* I feel my blood heat, my heart thudding in my chest. I scramble to shove a hand into my pocket, my eyes widening as I feel only dry crusted flakes.

"Boy, when I found you in the back of my wagon you looked worse than the wheel of cheese you crushed. Several broken bones, bleeding all over the place, shards of glass buried in your chest where you're patting now. I saved you from death. That's a lot more than helping," he said, leaning back against a log, slicing into an apple with his knife.

Shards of glass buried in my chest? My palms begin to sweat. *When I was attacked, they broke the vials.* I take several deep, intentional breaths, "Thank... Thank you for saving me. But... I really need to get back to Altha."

"Of course. As soon as you have covered the wheel of cheese you ruined, the water you drank, the use of my cart and of course, my protection fee. Until then you aren't going anywhere, oh and those costs will continue to build as we go." He bit off the last word, sinking his teeth into the apple rather than cutting another slice off.

The shadows are creeping in around me again, my heart racing. "I... don't have any coin... if you get me back to..."

Sarfu lets out a burst of air, "No coin? Service then." He stopped chewing, looking me over. His nose crinkles, "I'm not quite sure what yet, but we will find a way for you to pay your debt. For now, get some rest. We will be back on the road at dawn."

I lay myself down, rolling so my back is to Sarfu and his hound. *What am I going to do? I have to get back. I can't stay here.* My chest tightens, sweat pooling along my forehead. What little light was coming from the fire has been consumed by the darkness building around me.

Remember to count your breaths, focus on nothing else. Altha's voice echoes through my mind. Breathe, count the breaths.

One... Two... Three... Four... Five...

I follow her guiding memory. My heartbeat begins to slow. *I have to survive. One... Two... I have to get home. Three... Four... Five...* The shadows began to recede, my eyes becoming heavy. *I will make it home...*

I can hear wood grinding against wood as I come to. The glaring sun searing my eyes as I sit up. Sarfu is shifting something around in the smallest of the three carts that make up the walls of the camp. Sitting up and stretching my arms I note that while everything felt stiff, the pain was mostly gone now. The tight feeling reminds me of the mornings after a long run through the woods the night before.

"You're looking a lot less bruised today," Sarfu grunts out, hopping down from the cart.

"I feel much better, thanks," I say, my hand tracing the scab from where he had lanced my head.

"There won't be a scar. So don't bother thinking up a cool story to tell the girls when you get back," Sarfu said, before making a sharp whistle. I hear the thumping of paws before seeing the enormous wolf come galloping up next to him. All the while its green eyes are locked on me.

I can feel my heart begin to beat faster. *That's what was sleeping across from me? That is what he was petting so casually?* "What is that? I have never seen something that big before."

"She... is a dire wolf. I wouldn't suspect you see much of anything in that small hamlet of yours. Mindi here, has been with me since she was able to fit in the palm of my hand." He climbs into the smallest of the three carts, sitting on its bench before waving me up and patting the seat beside him.

I swallow hard, making sure to take a deep breath. *Breathe, you need to breathe, it's not going to hurt you.* "Mindi, your dire wolf, she found me in the cart?" I ask, climbing up beside him.

"Remember our little talk last night do you?" he muses, cracking the reins. The horses lurch the cart forward into a steady trot. "Good. That means you didn't hurt your head too badly. Yes, Mindi found you and made a mighty fuss. Not often something gets into one of my carts without Mindi catching it. Then again, you smelled horrible when we found you so maybe that kept her away."

The Nitpaw. "Did I happen to have any vials on me when you found me?"

His eyes tightened slightly, darting between me and the road. He lowers his hand, tugging a crossbow closer to him, "No. Lots of broken glass through."

My eyes linger on his hand, spotting the bolt already knocked in the crossbow. "Are you expecting trouble?" I ask, intentionally looking around us. The dirt road splits between the planes of grass, the beginnings of a forest a few miles off to the side.

Sarfu's eyes watch me sideways, his teeth ever so slightly creaking from pressure. "Trouble can be found in strange places out on the road. Sometimes it's bears, sometimes it's grown men, sometimes it's... *other* things. I prefer to be ready. Especially when I travel through this area." Sarfu lifts his fingers to his lips, letting out a sharp whistle that sends Mindi off at a full sprint. Chunks of mud flying through the air as her paws rip into the ground.

I turn around, looking back at the larger carts behind us. No additional horses pull them, no obvious point of attachment. Yet somehow they are following behind us at a mirrored pace and distance from one another. "How?" I whisper.

Sarfu's laughs. The sudden force of it causing me to flinch, my hands darting up for a second. My cheeks heat, realizing how ridiculous I look cowering at someone's laugh.

"I sometimes forget that Red River doesn't use even the simplest of magics. The carts are magically connected to each other. Where this one goes, the others follow. My people are experts at such things," Sarfu said.

It feels like a thousand spiders are crawling down my arms as I remember Altha's bedtime stories. Each one teaching the same lesson. *No magic is free, there is always a price to pay.* Then again, these carts didn't look or feel anything like her stories. No demons are coming to eat us. My skin wasn't being ripped from my bones. The sun wasn't turning crimson. In fact, I can't see the downside. Even the horses don't appear hindered. Even though it would be impossible for two horses to pull all three carts, especially as loaded as they are.

The hair on the back of my neck rises. I can faintly hear something over the sound of the cart's wheels sloshing through the muck beneath us.

"Stop," I said, my hand launching forward and gripping Sarfu's. His face tightens, pulling back the rains. The horses coming to a stop.

"What?" he asks.

"Shhh," I say, holding up a finger. I close my eyes, pushing the obvious sound away. It feels like minutes pass when I know it's only seconds as a howl tickles my ear. My eyes launch open, locked on the forest the howl originated from. I take in a deep breath, my bruised lungs aching from the attempt as I cough. I try again, this time a breeze sweeping by, bringing with it the subtle scent of wet fur. *Definitely a wolf...*

A hand grips my shoulder, my legs kicking back as I slide to the edge of the bench.

"Woah now, what made you so jumpy all the sudden?" Sarfu asks, his eyes drifting to the forest that I had been looking at a moment ago.

"I thought..." I start to say, looking back at the forest. *Would he believe me if I told him?*

"Thought what?" Sarfu said, his voice deepening ever so slightly.

"That I heard something."

"Did you now..." Sarfu said, rising to his feet. His eyes scan the tree line. His jaw as tight as stone. His knuckles shining white as the crossbow in his hand creaks under the pressure. "Well, we should be on our way to my next stop then." Thudding back on the seat before cracking the reins three times, sending the horses into a powerful galop that pressed my back into the seat.

The scent of sap and frost covered needles fills my nose as the chilled breeze slices through my thin, tattered clothes. The clouds stealing the slightest warmth the sun may have offered me. Sarfu shows no sign of discomfort, one hand still gripping the crossbow as we turn around a bend, entering a thicket of spruce trees.

My muscles relax a little, despite my nerves coursing with lightning.

It feels strange as we snake along the winding path with just enough room for Sarfu's large carts to make the turns. Almost as if this exact path was carved through the forest specifically for him.

The sound of tree branches shifting echoes from behind us, drawing my eyes. Sarfu grips my wrist, shaking his head slowly side to side, "Now you stay silent. Let me do the talking. These people like their privacy and can get aggressive at times."

Nodding, I look around again. More branches rustling all around us. I take a shallow sniff, unable to make out anything over the smell of the surrounding trees.

"It's me boys!" Sarfu shouts. "Don't go getting any ideas. Marcus won't be happy if I stop coming by."

"We will let him know you're here," A low male voice says from within the trees. He takes a loud, sharp sniff, "He won't be happy you brought a..."

"We will let him know you're here," A female voice interrupts. Followed by the sound of two people jogging away.

Sarfu's eyes travel over me, one eyebrow raised. The gesture sending a shiver down my already frozen spine. "Remember to stay quiet."

As we round the bend an enormous mansion comes into view. The winding path had clearly been cut away specifically to conceal the structure from anyone passing by. Though impressive in size, its window shutters are hanging at odd angles. Other windows are boarded up. The frame has slight cracks and all the wood looks as though it has weathered decades of harsh winters, despite the tree cover that the forest provides. A large fountain sits in front of the mansion's double doors. In its center, a statue of a horse rearing, jagged chunks of stone on its back from where a rider once was.

Sarfu brings the cart around the fountain, coming to rest just beyond the front doors. The doors slam open as we step down from the cart, a man dressed in a black leather trench coat that ends just above his knees and tattered pants smiling wide at Sarfu. His boots thud against the wooden deck as he storms into what little light shines through the trees. A tattoo of a bleeding heart wrapped in chains positioned on his chest. Every other inch of his skin has more muscle than even Sarfu has.

"Sarfu! My friend, it has been far too long since your last visit," the man exclaims, arms spread wide.

"Marcus. It's been no longer than normal," Sarfu replies, embracing him in a firm hug before patting him on the back.

"Really? Feels longer, what with these winters coming sooner and sooner am I right?" Marcus asks, looking at me with a slightly open jaw, his tongue pressing against his sharp canine. "And where did you pick up this stray?"

"Found him nearly dead, hidden away in one of my carts if you can believe that," Sarfu said, letting out a low chuckle.

I can feel Marcus's eyes linger on me, the air becoming still and heavy. "Well, why don't I have the boys pull my cargo and we can talk about it inside, yes? It's a bit chilly out here after all," Marcus says With a snap of his fingers, six large, similarly built men dressed in various tattered clothes come rushing out of the mansion, grabbing things from each cart with little to no effort.

Sarfu grips my shoulder, guiding me toward the door. The inside of the mansion is a little better than the outside. Torn carpets, nearly every wooden wall has gouges. Worst of all is the smell, overpowering every other scent, *wet fur*. I look up to Sarfu, covering my nose as he glances my way.

"Marcus homes a lot of animals. Keeps them from getting out of hand in the forest, that way I can travel safely through it."

Marcus glances over his shoulder at me but continues walking into the next room. "Yes, well, I wouldn't call them *animals* but they are very important to me. Misunderstood by most, feared by others." Marcus pushes open a door, gesturing inside. "The boy can wait in here while we talk business Sarfu, we have sensitive matters to discuss after all."

My teeth click together as my eyes dart between Sarfu and the room, my calves tightening. My body and mind are already aware of what I am just now understanding. *Something isn't right.* "I..."

"That won't be a problem," Sarfu said, his glaring eyes telling me to get in the room.

I take a step forward, peering into the room. A single worn table and chair sit against the far wall below a battered boarded up window. A single burning candle, the only light source in the room. "I would prefer..." I begin to say.

"I have business to get done. Call this your job for the day and I will say you paid for the food and drink last night," Sarfu interrupted, shoving me forward.

I stumble on stiff legs into the room, catching myself on the wooden table as the door slams shut behind me. My stomach tightens as I hear a bolt sliding, clicking into place. I rush to the door, pulling hard despite already knowing. *Locked.*

I rush to the window, tugging on the well-secured boards. *Trapped. Alone.* The shadows in the corners of the room seem ready to pounce. Barely being held back by the flickering light of the candle. I collapse into the chair, the wood creaking ready to give way at any moment. I push my shaking hands together. *No!* I ball my hands into fists. My nails dig into my palms, sending bolts of pain shooting up to my shoulders as droplets of blood drip onto the floor. I hear each droplet land against the boards beneath me, my world slowing to a crawl.

I take a deep breath, "One..." I count. "Two... Three... Four... Five..." I continue, counting each breath. My heartbeat slows, my muscles loosening as the sound of blood flowing through my ears fades away. I focus my mind, hearing muffled words from the next room. I slowly rise to my feet, pressing my ear to the wall.

"You're telling me that he had this on him?" Marcus asks.

"By the amount of broken glass I pulled from his pockets, he had a handful, but that was the only one left," Sarfu said.

"Where did he come from?"

"You know I can't tell you that."

"Don't you play that game with me Sarfu. You are the one that brought that stray into my land. What if others come looking for him? After you have gone on your merry way."

"I camped for two days after finding him, no one came looking. I even sent Mindi out. Nothing. No one is gonna come looking after I leave."

"Fine. You. Move it to the caves. How much extra do I owe you, and remember that I am not paying for...."

The sound of the latch being pulled has me scrambling back just before the door bursts open slamming against the wall. Two men rush into the room, their eyes glowing. I stumble back further, falling to the ground.

They storm over to me as I continue to try to get away on all fours, my feet unable to grip against the floor as I try to feel for anything to use as a weapon. My head crashes into the corner of the room, sending tingles of warmth down my neck. "I'm with Sar..." a fist connects with my head collapsing my world into darkness.

Metal crashing against metal fills my ears as I rise from the wet stone beneath me. "Where are you from?" a deep raspy voice asks.

The smell of sweat, dirt and wet fur fills my nose as I take in the man behind the metal bars. His boots are worn and caked in dry mud, his pants shredded at the knees, yet his white shirt is crisp and clean, almost as if brand new.

"Where are you from?" the man said again, dragging a metal rod across the bars.

The air feels heavy as I try to look up at his eyes, unable to get above his neckline. My muscles scream. Begging me to get lower, to become smaller.

The metal rod clangs along the bars again, "Where are you from?" The air, made even heavier by his words.

I open my mouth, attempting to speak yet only a shallow squeak escapes my lips. My hands slam against my chest, nails tearing through my shirt. My lungs feel ready to burst, my face slamming against the ground. An airless gasp erupting from my throat, my chest arching forward.

"Pitiful," the man said, spitting at the ground. His boots scrape against the stone, getting farther away with each step.

After the fifth step the air begins to thin, life crawling into my lungs once more.

"Slow and steady, it might take a minute to get your bearings," a warm, gentle voice says.

Panting, I raise my head, meeting the jade eyes of the frail young women in the cell next to mine. Her fingers, barely poking out from her worn leather jacket, are wrapped around the bars.

"I think he is used to people jumping to answer his questions, and got a little upset when you sat there, silent as a newborn pup. So how did they catch you?"

"I was locked in a room." My hand caressing my throat as I take my first deep breath. "How about you?"

"Oh they spotted me trying to pocket some of the meat from that creepy orcs wagon," she said with a giggle. "I'm Alice by the way, and you are?"

"Alex," I said, clearing my throat.

"Well, Alex, at least we have company while stuck in a hole underground," she says, tilting her head back slightly. The tiny bit of moonlight creeping into the cave shimmers off her eyes, for a moment I swear they were glowing.

I press off my knees, rising to my feet. My hair brushes the stone ceiling as each new bruise makes themselves known. I approach the bars. Despite the stone floor, each step feels like trudging through river muck. "The air feels strange," I said, resting my head against the bars as I stare down the single dark path out of the room. My mind replays the man's footsteps as they clacked against the stone. My heartbeat increases, the pace between my breaths along with it. *Must survive, must escape.*

"I don't feel anything," Alice said.

I stumble back, slamming my head against the ceiling. I hiss, heat building within my hands with each second, my muscles tightening.

"Ouch, are you ok?" As she spoke a breeze swept over me. My shoulders rolling back, hands slowly falling to my side. My blood cools, a peace that I have only felt while deep in the forest, under the full moon. "Here, let me see." Her silk smooth hands extended through the bars, beckoning me closer.

I feel lighter than ever, taking a single step into her silky hands.

She clicks her tongue as she gently begins petting my hair. "There, there, you're ok, just breathe." Once again, a blanket of peace wraps around me. Stronger than before, images of the forest flashing through my mind. "We are ok, just breathe, breathe with me."

One... Two...

CHAPTER 3

The white marble beneath my feet flows up into giant columns. Supporting the great slab ceiling of the marketplace. I can already feel the throbbing in my head as we maneuver through the crowds of elves, constantly shifting between the minds of everyone around Prince Viccar taking its toll.

Today marks two years serving as his Mindblade. I have never glimpsed a single negative thought in his direction. On the contrary, his people adored him, cherishing any interaction they had with him.

Far more pleasant than the terror that ripples through their minds the moment they notice me. His ever-present shadow, draped from head to toe in gray robes, leaving only my sunset orange eyes visible. The winter breeze pushes against the thick fabric. Perhaps the only benefit of the garb is the protection it provides from the winter air.

Prince Viccar comes to a smooth stop, his golden embroidered white robes barely shifting as he caresses the ornate fabric tapestry before him. The vendor gives a deep bow before going over its fine qualities. Having already confirmed that this vendor also loved his prince, I reached out with my mind, touching the bridge that connects me to Iromae, my ever vigilant Shadow Guard.

Entering someone's mindscape is simple enough. Navigating or remaining undetected is quite another story. The mind has a way of protecting itself, building up landscapes that often reflect who the person is. Iromae's mindscape is a clear representation of her razor sharp focus, snowdrifts sweep across its vast planes, instantly erasing my footsteps.

"Are you cold?" my thoughts echo through her mind.

Iromae's response sent wisps of snow bounding toward me, gently pushing me back to the bridge. *"You should be focused on the Prince, as I am focused on you."* The chill from her mindscape follows me back across the bridge, watching over me, even in my own mind.

Prince Viccar is still haggling with the vendor and appears to be narrowing down its final price.

I cast out a thin connection to several elves that had come near the stall, all of which were focused either on the fabrics on display or the thrill that their Prince was before them. I catch a wisp of deceit from the merchant across the way, turning my entire focus upon him.

"It is of the finest quality threads. I spun each of them myself, you will not find one of better quality, I assure you," the merchant said, his ring covered hands dancing along the tapestries surface. I tug on my connection to his mind, images floating to me of his wife pulling threads together from several torn tapestries. All while he sat upon a bed of pillows, drinking the night away.

Everyone lies.

I reach out to the prospective customer's mind. Feeling his uncertainty at the tapestry's quality. I merge our minds for the briefest of moments, lifting his hand and twisting the tapestry's edges between two fingers. Drifting from his mind as quickly as I arrived.

"Perhaps if you were to lower your price, I would overlook the recycled threads," the customer said, looking at the merchant with a grin of victory.

I turn back to my Prince, just as he clasps arms with the man he had been haggling with. "We are in agreement then, have it delivered to the palace tonight," Prince Viccar's warm voice boomed.

The marble stairs sparkle under the moon's rays as I ascend a few steps behind Prince Viccar. The enormous doors of the palace come into view. Their sheer size, more suited to something far larger than the elves that reside within. Four gray-skinned orcs pull the doors open. Their bulging muscles are barely concealed by the thin silk fabric of white draped over them. Silver embroidery dancing across its edges placing them among the palace's servant class.

While still among the servant class they take great pride in those white fabrics. Often entire families spend generations to gain position with the palace walls. Between not knowing my parents and my half-elf blood, the inner palace would be forever out of my reach. In fact, if not for my Mindblade abilities I would have been lucky to have just survived.

I kneel before my Prince as he vanishes behind the enormous doorway. The orcs pushing the doors closed with an audible *thud*. A gentle hand presses atop my shoulder, my aching legs straining to rise. My eyes follow along the hand, covered in the pure black leathers of the Shadow Guard before meeting Iromae's smiling green eyes. "I will never understand how you can approach so undetected," I say in greeting, my smile hidden by the gray fabric.

The rough leathers she wears absorb all light, yet they leave nothing to the imagination. Molded around her toned muscles, earned from decades of training. A sharp contrast to my own slender form. My training had been focused solely on sharpening my mind rather than my body. Mindblades are rare after all, even among the pure blood Elven Lords of Everenthia.

A breeze floats through my mind. *"The city looks beautiful tonight, my lady,"* Iromae's thoughts vibrate through my mind with the sweet undertone that betrays the lethal training I know she has.

No matter how many times I see it I can't stop the smile from forming, the warmth from building in my chest. I can see the entire city from atop the palace steps. Everenthia rests on the edge of a cliff that overlooks the never-ending sea. The palace rests at the peak, surrounded by the merchant lords. Their mansions, each one encased within their own protective walls with guards atop their battlements. Just beyond them rests the grand market-places of marble, its polished surface sparkles under the moonlight. The inner layer is surrounded by thick walls which house battalions of skilled elven archers. Beyond them is a labyrinth of stone and wood. The home of Everenthia's military and servant class, surrounded by yet another enormous wall with yet more battlements.

A single tear rolls down my cheek. While those outside the inner-city dream of being let in, I dream of finally leaving it.

Another tug within my mind, *"Seal off your mind my lady, even I should not have free passage to your thoughts,"* Iromae's voice whispers within my mind. Normally she can't touch the minds of others, but I keep the bridge open between us. While she has never liked it, it brings me a sense of comfort. If the bridge is still there, she is alive. My one and only friend in my small world.

We stand in silence for a few moments while I put up the weakest of barriers between the bridge connecting our minds. She won't feel the disconnect, but I will still feel the comfort of its presents. "It is beautiful..." I say, never looking away from the vast world beyond those walls.

The orbs of light float mere inches above our heads, our only source of light as we make our way through the tunnels carved into the very sandstone bedrock that supports the palace above. Iromae and I had been granted only a few moments to enjoy the wondrous view of the world only to then be torn away by Mentor Morvina's summons.

Mentor Morvina sends a chill down my spine on good days. She isn't a Mindblade herself. No, instead she is gifted with great magic that is suited only for war. Despite that, she taught me how to control my thoughts. How to peer into the minds of others without being noticed. What I had glimpsed within her mind had terrified me beyond measure. Watching, as if through my own eyes, thousands of soldiers have their bones ripped from their bodies, only for them to turn and begin fighting their brothers in arms.

"Take a seat," Morvina commands before we even round the corner into her office. Tonight, she is wearing a white robe that flows down to just above the ground. Not a single spec of dust present as she leans over a small replica of Everenthia that sprawls the length of the large stone table in the center of the room. Large bookshelves lining the walls, filled with ancient tomes of past battles.

I obey without a word, taking the nearest wooden stool beside the great table alongside Iromae.

Morvina's elven muscles have a youthful glow despite her true age. She has lived through the Great Tear after all. Today marks one thousand years since King Glanduil, Prince Viccar's father, had gathered the other Kings. Together they banished Dracordian within the deep fissure, along with the entire human kingdom. The humans that remained believed it to be too great a price, but they had brought it upon themselves. Summoning such a demon to the surface world.

Morvina had taken the intrusion into that specific memory personally, despite her having demanded that I was not tearing through her barriers properly. My hands and back ache as the memory of being forced to scrub the entire tunnel we had just walked through with a single bucket and brush over the course of several months.

"Tomorrow Prince Viccar will be walking the streets of the military ward. Here, just outside the inner wall," Morvina says, pointing with the tip of her dagger. Her yellow eyes rise, meeting mine with a stare that stiffens my spine. "People beyond the walls of Everenthia will be present. Despite this, the Prince wishes to show strength."

I can feel my nails digging into my palms as I try desperately to contain my excitement at going beyond the inner walls. It must show in my eyes as Morvina continues to lock eyes with me, her lips tightening to a thin line. "I expect you to remain focused and keep your prince safe, Mindblade."

I have never been sure if she was unaware of my name or just refused to use it. "Of course, Mentor," I said, bowing my head, if only to avert her gaze.

"Iromae, three additional Shadow Guards will be assigned to protect Prince Viccar. Here are their names,"

Morvina said, passing a slip of paper to Iromae. "While their focus will be on protecting Prince Viccar, you will continue to guard the Mindblade."

Iromae glances at the note before sliding back to Morvina, "As you command, Mentor."

The heavy gray robes fall from my shoulders to the smooth floor of my room. Letting out a drawn-out sigh of relief as I free my blonde hair. Allowing it to fall free for the first time since this morning.

I collapse onto my plush bed, one of the few benefits of my position. I stretch my limbs out, bunch up my soft wool blankets against the wall as an aching pleasure ripples from each of my joints.

I can barely hear the servant's feet move outside my door over the sound of my beating heart. *Tomorrow I will be stepping beyond the inner walls.* I could barely contain my excitement as Morvina went over tomorrow's plan. I can remember the first few paths that the Prince will take but quickly find myself envisioning what it would look like, smell like, *feel* like to be outside those walls in my own skin.

Lucky for me, my duties are simple enough that I can repeat it by memory, especially since they never change. *Follow ten steps behind Prince Viccar and enter every mind he approaches.*

Iromae would have heard the whole plan anyway. Since Morvina would look to Iromae before moving onto the next phase of the route. My input was never requested, nor needed when it came to plans for the day.

I close my eyes, reaching out with my mind to feel for those beyond my walls. The world falls away as I let my energy float through the upper levels, up to the towers that look out over the city. I find the archer's mind quiet and relaxed. I slowly weave my energy around his mind, gently forming the connection.

While Iromae has a snow-covered landscape, the archers mind is that of shifting desert sands. I take a calm step forward. My toes digging into the sand, waiting for any hint that he would be aware of my presence. *Nothing.*

I step fully within his mind leaving a tether back to my connection point.

Never enter a mind without a path out. Morvina had told me so many times during our training.

With my tether in place, I close my eyes again. Though I could still feel the warmth of my room, the softness of my bed beneath me, my eyes now see through his. Looking out over the sprawling city, quiet in the dead of night. He slowly scans the land. It always feels strange, unlike mine, fully elven eyes are capable of focusing on things miles away. Almost as if he can fly across the city within an instant to observe another guard taking his post, only to be back atop his tower a moment later.

I reach out, gently pushing a suggestion through his mind that something had moved off to the right along the wall. His eyes dart upon that spot, focusing so close that I could make out the soot along its surface. Satisfied that he must have seen a shadow he looks up, taking in the full moon glinting off the ocean's surface.

I tug the tether connecting me home and float like a breeze out of his mind, cutting the connection on my way out. The plain slab walls of my room crashing down around me once more. *Tomorrow...* tomorrow I won't need to look out through another's eyes. I will be able to walk through the streets, and see it with my own.

Ice clings to the air as it whips against my heavy gray robes. Countless people surround our path, shouting their love for Prince Viccar.

We finally reach the large iron gates, the sounds of chains clanging together sound from within the walls as it begins to rise, only increasing the throbbing in my head. Normally I would have saved most of my mental energy for beyond these gates, but the Prince stopped more times than I can count. Shaking the hands of beautiful ladies, or kissing the foreheads of babies. Each of them swooning for his attention.

I can feel the eyes of the archers above us watch every step as we step beyond the walls. The military ward's path is lined every ten feet with a roaring brazier that battles back the falling snow. Guards adorned with form-fitting metal armor line the path. Each of them holding a long spear pointed to the sky behind bronze shields embroidered with the Everenthia crest, a longbow draped over a crescent moon.

The worn down wooden structures are joined together by makeshift bridges that seem to float overhead, leaving only small sections of the sky visible at any one time.

A chill runs down my spine at the realization that I have not been checking the minds of the people we pass. I recklessly push out connections to several of the guards ahead and all those immediately around us. The first batch feels strange, like stepping out onto a frozen lake, water barely flowing beneath its thin surface.

The hair along my arms rises, not feeling even the smallest flutter of thought within their minds. Even with Iromae's trained calmness I would see a thought float through her mind when she would spot a shadow move, or a leaf float too close to me. Their minds feel empty, like that of a corpse.

We continue down the path, each of the guard's minds are the same, void of emotion or thought. We round a corner and I spot what appears to be a younger guard, his armor slightly too large for his frame.

The Prince stops before him, his hands balling into fists. He tilts his head to the slide, a single eyebrow raised.

Within his mind I feel the ground quake, fear and panic flowing like rapids through the air. The word 'no' echoing through his mind over and over as the space between the words shrinks.

The sound of metal clanging through the air, followed by a bone-chilling silence. My toe strikes a bit of stone, pulling me out of the boy's mind as I stumble forward, my eyes widening in fear. Something arrests my fall, pulling at my robes just in time to prevent me from crashing into the Prince. I look over my shoulder, relief sweeping over me only to find nothing there. A wisp of cold twists across the bridge that connects me to Iromae, *"Stay focused my lady."*

I quickly regain my position behind the Prince. His scowling eyes locked on the trembling boy kneeling before him, his shield now laying on the ground several feet away. *Had he not noticed my stumble?*

I feel a sense of panic building within me as Prince Viccar's eyes burn into the boy's back. *The connection!* In my blunder I left my connection to the boy open. I quickly sever the thin strand between us, the roaring panic falling away with it.

I let out a silent sigh, feeling a slight tug within my mind. Instinct has me looking to my bridge with Iromae, yet it was clear... no whispers of snow.

"How very interesting... I wonder if you even know what it is that you are," a grave, bodiless voice hisses, its words echoing throughout my mind.

My heart stopped beating, my muscles screaming as they tensed without my instruction. *I can't control my body.*

In my mindscape a deep tar-like ooze drips all around me. Forming into obsidian pillars of stone that form walls, encasing me. *Trapping me.* I will myself forward but my legs refuse to respond, my screams silent as my throat tears itself under the effort.

"Shall I show you what you're capable of me dear?" the bodiless voice asks.

It's as though I am looking through someone else's eyes. My hands flex before me, blue crackling light sparking from my palms. My fingers begin to rotate and dance, the sparks fusing together into a blue crackling sphere floating between my palms.

"My lady?" Iromae's voice whispers through my mind.

"Stop... me..." I push the words across the bridge. Blood pouring out of my nose, my heart searing in pain. I feel our

bridge shatter like glass, my world crumbling with it as my last line of hope falls into the endless void.

"How interesting that you would openly keep a connection to another. It was so entrenched I believed it part of your mindscape itself. No matter."

I can feel my hands burning from the energy between them as the sphere expands. It's as if Prince Viccar were moving in slow motion as he turns toward me, the hazel in his eyes barely visible as his eyes widen. A single bead of sweat crawls down his face. I feel my arms flex, palms moving apart as something kicks my knee. Simultaneously a palm slams into my face, throwing me into the cobblestone path just as the sphere is launched forward. It grazes the Prince's hair before colliding with the building behind him.

Ringing fills my ears as control returns to my limbs. I roll, putting my hands underneath me. Tears flood down my face as a burst of air explodes from my smoke-filled lungs. The building the sphere had struck was gone, along with the two buildings to either side. It was as if the sphere had expanded upon impact, erasing everything it touched. In its place, a perfectly smooth upside-down dome shaped crater in the earth.

I hear muffled words as the ringing in my ears begins to subside. Searching for the source, I find several guards rising to their feet, raising their spears toward me. My eyes widen, taking in more of my surroundings.

They think it was me. "I... where is the Prince?" I ask.

"Safe. No thanks to you, traitorous *witch*," Morvina says, her words dripping with venom.

Before I can turn around, her arm is locked around my throat. Squeezing as she pulls me off my feet. I desperately gasp for air, my legs thrashing, nails digging into her arm. I push into Morvina's mind but a terrifying wall of black fire blocks my connection.

"Such a waste. You could..." the grave, hissing voice sounded through my mind before I felt the connection break suddenly. A band snaps around my neck sending searing pain through my head. I collapse to the ground screaming before darkness takes me.

Chapter 4

The room feels fuzzy as I pull my eyes open. The cold iron shackles digging into my wrists as I dangle against the sandstone wall with my knees floating inches from the floor. I take a long steady breath, sliding my bare feet under me.

The small room is similarly carved as the tunnels beneath the palace, a single slab bench juts out from the opposite wall. A single wooden door off to one side.

My mind is quiet, a silence I have not felt since before my gifts manifested. It feels as though the entire world beyond these walls died. *Or perhaps I am the one that died.*

I attempt to yell out, my voice cracking as pain tears along my dry throat. I take in my tattered and singed robes. Streaks of blood stain its surfaces.

I pull my chains, their rattling echoing off the walls.

The still silence of the room sends a chill down my spine as goosebumps sweep across my aching arms. *When was the last time I was alone, truly alone? Before Iromae there was Morvina, before her...* My head begins to throb even harder. I take a deep breath, letting the pain drift out with each breath. *I can't remember before her.*

I flex my hands over and over in time with each of my breaths. Forcing my mind center on the here and now. I can feel the band that Morvina placed around my neck tighten with each breath, the rough material rubbing my skin raw.

I pull my thoughts in, entering my mindscape. Complete emptiness is all I can see. No whispers floating through the air. No snow drifts brushing out from the rubble that was once the bridge connecting Iromae and myself.

I drift to it, picking up one of the frost covered bricks. It is warm to the touch despite its outward appearance. *So much like her.* I turn, searching through my mind for anything, any sign of the outside world. The dark walls from the intruder are gone. Not even a speck of their vile chill remains. While Iromae's bridge has left the smallest remnants, it is as if he had never been here at all. Somehow that only causes me to feel more uneasy. As if there is a wrongness within my mind now that I am unable to see.

I allow my mind to drift, a gentle current taking me where it may. Perhaps my subconscious mind is aware of something my conscious mind is not.

What feels like hours pass with no signs of the outside world, no whispers of the past. My headache begins to numb, the darkness of my mind's floor turning to a grassy green as I come to a stop. I squint, rubbing my eyes as I try to make out the blurry blob of greens, yellows and browns that were now before me. *What is this?* I reach out cautiously.

What feels like a bubble bursts as tingling energy rushes up my arm. The colors begin to shift and pull. Warping the space around me, grass begins to tickle my feet as it grows. I take several steps back, only stopping only once my feet are back on the solid emptiness of my mind once more.

As I looked back at what was once a blob of color I gasp, taking in the stone bridge before me. Moss grows out from between the cracks. Vines with beautiful white and yellow flowers blooming off them are wrapped around its frame, binding the various stones together. As if nature itself had formed the bridge.

I push a thread out, tasting the energy of the connection. It doesn't feel the same as the wall, not an intrusion. No this has been here for so long I can feel bits of myself in it. The energy feels ancient, as though it had been with me since before I took my first breath.

Where do you lead? I suddenly find myself stepping onto the bridge, the stone feeling as though it had sat in the sun all day. A gentle breeze brushes across my face that reminds of the morning air floating up across the ocean.

I open my eyes, no longer in my mindscape, but in someone else's. Moonlight trickles through the tree canopy overhead, its gentle light bouncing off the grass and leaves that surround me.

A fawn steps out from behind a set of trees, looking... not at me, *through* me. My heart stilling with wonder at its beauty, its innocence.

"Hello?" I say, slowly reaching out my hand.

The fawn's ears shoot up, its head snapping from side to side as if searching for the sound.

"It's ok." My hand now inches from its brown and white fur.

A branch snaps from a nearby bush, echoing through the now still forest. The fawn sprints in the opposite direction, vanishing within seconds as an enormous black wolf slowly steps out of the bush. Its glowing blue eyes lock onto me.

I step to the side, its head tracking my movement.

A deep growl emanates from the wolf, the sound vibrating off my skin, *my bones*. I take another step back, keeping my eyes locked with the wolf.

A stone slips under my feet causing me to stumble back. I twist myself around, my arm scraping against a prickle bush just as the wolf snarls and leaps toward me.

I cry out, rolling over and throwing my arms in front of my face. The sound of rattling chains echo around me. My throat suddenly feels like it's on fire again. I lower my arms slowly, my heart pounding in my ears. My eyebrows pinch together taking in the sandstone room around me once again. A sharp pain slices down my arm, pulling my gaze. My heart stills, the room somehow going more silent as I watch blood drip from the shallow cut down my arm.

What feels like hours pass, listening to the sound of my breath. Rather than standing, I have chosen to remain hanging from my wrists, finding an angle that doesn't cause the shackles to dig into my skin but still allows me to relax.

I have scoured my mind for that moss covered bridge with no luck. Instead, I find myself reliving the attack on the Prince over and over. To have met someone with my abilities, only to then be attacked by them. Used as a weapon against my Prince.

They had to have been from another kingdom, but who would want to harm Everenthia? The people of Everenthia love their Prince. The humans depend on our kingdom for land and food. The orcs continually trade with us for our vibrant ores.

It could be the fairies... No one has heard from them since the Great Tear. Hidden away in their dense forests, whispering promises of wealth and power. Only to then drain the life from those that enter.

The latch to my door sides open as I rush to my feet. The heavy door swinging wide to reveal Morvina, her face pinched as she glares down at me. She is dressed in her red tunic that ends just above her knees. A small dagger attached to a black belt that is perfectly wrapped around her waist.

Iromae stands behind her, just off to the side wearing her all black leathers.

The air feels thick as they enter the room, my stomach turning over as I relive memories of my past failures. How Morvina *smiled* while punishing us for them.

"You traitorous witch," Morvina said through gritted teeth, slapping me across the face. The force sends me toward the floor, the chains digging into my wrists as they arrest my fall. "You don't get to look me in the eye after what you did," She says as I hear her adjust her belt.

I keep my eyes low, sliding my feet under me again. My raw skin begging for relief, "Mentor." My throat burns, cutting my words off as it constricts so hard that I can't even breathe. My eyes widen, feeling as if they will burst.

"Mentor please..." I hear Iromae say.

Morvina chuckles. Her heels clack against the stone as I feel my throat loosen, allowing me to gasp for air.

"You also do not get to speak to me. I will not hear the poisonous words of one that would betray their kingdom. After everything they did for you. You were nothing, less than nothing. They gave you purpose, a place to belong. All you had to do was remain loyal," Morvina said.

I could hear the tension in her voice. I have to be careful. She is already on the edge, but I need to tell her. *I need her to know it wasn't me.* "Ment..."

The blow came so fast that I felt the pain in my head before feeling the blow itself. "I told you not to speak!" Morvina said, spitting on me. "I don't have the patience for this any longer. Iromae, you may have your moment with the traitor, but only a moment. I will not have her waste any more of my time than she already has."

I hear Morvina's heavy steps end just outside the room, just as Iromae's feet appear on the ground in front of me. Her hand gently coming to rest on my shoulder.

"I know that this wasn't you," Iromae whispers.

My eyes shoot up, filled with tears as they meet hers.

"Shhhh, shhhh. Don't speak, Mentor has forbidden it and I do not wish to see you harmed further. We are about to go to the Hall of Trust, it is very important that while inside you speak only when questioned. The council is less reserved than the Mentor, the truth will be revealed regardless of if you speak once inside."

Less reserved? My spine tightens at the thought of Morvina being the example of restraint.

"I will enter the hall first. Know that the stories you have heard of the hall are true, but that not all of the truth has been shared. The servants are sworn to secrecy before they enter. I believe that this will be the last time I am to see you, my lady."

My heart stills as I see the honesty in her face.

"I want you to know that I do not hold you accountable, nor do I wish ill upon you. My time as your ward, as your friend, has been an honor. I do not know what happened out there, but I know that you are not to blame."

A tear runs down my check. Iromae gently brushes it away with her thumb. I push my check against her hand, embracing her silk touch.

Nearly an hour has passed while Morvina and I stand before the enormous doors of the Hall of Truth. Ancient elvish runes carved into the solid sandstone block glow with a gentle white light that feels like the morning sun.

Prior to this moment I had only received glimpses of this place. Few minds of those I touched had ever seen it, but never had they shown me beyond these great doors. Some indicated that this place was built long before the elves arrived. That we merely took it over from those before. Others said after the Great Tear the old ones themselves forged this space. Their desire, for those found guilty to never feel the warmth of the sun again. Regardless, the Hall of Truth is a place of great power to our people. Its location is a closely guarded secret.

Soon I would enter these ancient halls, in chains and filthy tattered robes. I try to hold onto some dignity and remain on my own two feet, each of my muscles throbbing, as though I were swimming through a pool of needles.

Morvina has not spoken a word since we arrived. Simply standing as if made of stone. I flinch, my muscles screaming at the sudden movement as the doors begin to swing in. Warm light along with the sound of muffled chatter spilling through the doorway.

A slender elf dressed in the purest of white robes steps out, his face obscured under a white hood. "The council will see you now," he said. His voice is absent of emotion as he gives a shallow nod, raising an impossibly white hand toward the door.

Morvina bows deeply. Slowly rising before marching toward the room with a hard pull on the chain. I stumble forward, landing hard on my face with an audible *crunch* followed by pain lancing through my eyes and up into my forehead.

"Stupid girl!" Morvina screeched. Storming to me, her heels sound like thunder striking the ground.

"Hold," the man said. A wave of energy ripples through the room. I look up to see Morvina completely frozen mid step.

A cough has me looking down again, seeing my blood smeared on the ground. I look back at Morvina, her eyes filled with rage that makes my blood freeze.

"Look upon me, one that is to be judged," the man says.

Every one of my bones burn as I get to my knees, blood flowing freely down my face as I look under his hood. His skin is equally as white as his robes, as if he has never experienced the warmth of the sun. His eyes were the opposite. Black as the night sky, completely void of stars. His right hand snaps up, fingers outstretched as he begins chanting a language that feels old. Small golden spheres of light appear at the tip of his fingers before floating to me. Their warmth soaking into my skin, the pain flowing away like a breeze.

"Thank you," I whisper, bowing my head. My eyes pinch tight, noticing that all the blood that was on the floor was now gone as well. My robes, more pristine than the day I first received them.

"Rise now, and enter the hall," the man said.

I push my legs up, ready for pain that never comes. I look at the robed man in wonder but he remains unmoving. His raised arm silently ushering me through the door.

"Thank you," I whisper again, a tear trailing down my face as I walk through the doors.

Stepping across the threshold sends tingles up my arms. The very air vibrating with the same energy I felt from the robed man outside. An inaudible gasp fills my chest as my eyes adjust, taking in the beautiful space before me. Polished marble floors seamlessly merge into the naturally grown crystal cluster walls. At the far end is another large door, this one made of obsidian with golden inlaid handles.

Finally, my eyes come to rest upon the council. Warmth fills my heart seeing Prince Viccar dressed in his formal robes of jade, the material shimmering against the faintest light as he sits in his simple redwood chair. Its frame is large enough to comfortably hold him, yet short enough to not overshadow the room. He appears relaxed, not even a hair out of place as his hazel eyes watch me come to a stop in the center of the room where Morvina forces me to my knees.

Queen Aredhel has not taken her eyes from her nails. Her jade dress leaves little to the imagination, revealing much of her tanned skin. She rests atop silk maroon pillows, draping over the side of her granite throne.

King Glanduil appears half interested as he sits upon his throne. This one appears to have been grown from the very crystals in this room. He wears simple white robes accented by slashes of jade, a delicate coronet of gold atop his long, shimmering brown hair.

The sandstone doors slam shut. Draping the room in silence as the robed man glides across the floor, his robes flowing with the smooth movement before stopping before me. His form nearly hiding me from the council's site. "Before you is the one that is to be judged. Ask your three questions and know the truth." His voice echoes with a power, the crystals along the walls vibrating with each word.

"Why did she attempt to kill my son?" King Glanduil asks, his voice smooth and gentle despite his age.

The man raises his hands to either side. I feel my chest rise, my mind becoming light.

"She did not attempt to kill your son," the man said.

The King's eyes tighten, his hands threading together as he leans forward.

"She launched some spell that vaporized an entire house!" the Queen voice shrills. "If not to kill him, what was she doing?"

I once again feel my chest rise, my mind lightening. My eyes dart up to the man at the realization that he was entering my mind somehow. I fumble to find my center, forcing the void of my mindscape to become present but find... *nothing*. No presence... just me.

"She was fighting for control of her mind while another cast the void sphere," the man said, pulling my focus back to the room.

The King's fists crash against his throne, "You wasted a question in your fit of rage!" His voice, void of the gentleness it contained moments ago. "Remain silent and do not speak again until I have asked the final one."

Minutes seem to pass, without a single word spoken. I swear that I can hear the sound of my heart beating in my chest as the King ponders his final question with his fingers once more intertwined.

"What is the true name of the one responsible for the attack on my son?"

A thrum of energy surges through the room. My chest feels a pull harder than before. Practically lifting me off the ground as the air in the room vibrates and crackles. My palms slap against the floor as a breeze sweeps through the room.

As the man speaks the lights in the room dim for a moment, the air becoming thick with death. "Ogroz Shoddlec of the Damned."

Several whispers echo through the room. The king's eyebrows pinching together.

"He can't possibly be alive, can he?" the Queen asks.

The man folds his arms behind him, pushing his hands into his sleeves. "Three questions, three answers. Your judgment?"

"Innocent," the King proclaims. My entire body relaxing into the floor as a smile pulls at my cheeks.

"NO!" the Queen screeches, her feet slamming against the floor. Pillows tumble to the ground around her. "She has to be punished for what she tried to do!"

"You heard the Old One. She was not in control of her actions at that time," the King says, his tone neutral yet firm.

The Old One. My entire spine locks, my eyes opening so wide that I can see either door while still staring straight down at the floor. It is said that the Old Ones were among the first to arrive in our world. One for each race. Their soul jumping to a new host upon their current one's death. Being a Mindblade was barely a fragment of the elven Old

Ones gifts. If this is the elven Old One, that would make him...

"Family," a voice more ancient than time itself echoes through my mind.

I rub the cold sweat from my palms, my lungs refusing to pull in air.

"That doesn't mean she shouldn't be punished. She was meant to protect our son, instead she allowed another to control her. Allowed them to make an attempt on his life. She nearly allowed our son to..." The Queen's sobs cut her off. But her message was clear, she wants someone to pay. Not someday, but here and now, she has chosen me. Regardless of what has been or would be said in this room.

The King pinches his nose between two fingers with a heavy sigh, "Very well, she will be executed at dawn."

Morvina steps forward, "My King. If I may speak?"

The King stills, looking through his fingers, "Proceed."

"The Mindblade came to us young. She is still young, and has not yet served Your Majesty enough to make up for her upbringing. Nor enough to make up for her failure two nights ago."

Two nights? Had I been asleep that long?

"If it pleases you, my Queen. I would request that instead of death, that the Mindblade be marked and sent to the mines. There she can pay her debt to the crown, to her kingdom." Even with her back to me, I could feel the joy oozing from Morvina with each word.

A terrifying grin crawls across the Queen's face, "I approve of this. It will serve as an example to others."

"It is done then. Get her out of my sight. We have much to discuss," the King states with a wave of his hand.

The robed man floats to the obsidian doorway, effortlessly opening the enormous door with the palm of his hand. Morvina pulls me to my feet, the sound of the chains rattling through the chamber. I lock eyes with the Prince, pleading for him to say something, *anything*. Yet all I receive is a cold, emotionless, stare as he watches me exit the room.

"Survive, young one," the ancient voice whispered in my mind. My heart tearing open as the obsidian doors slam shut.

A single, narrow stairwell shrouded in darkness is our only path forward. Faint light shines out from stones at the base of each step.

"Move," Morvina commands, shoving me into a stumble. I crash against the wall, my nails breaking as I claw for a hold, barely stopping myself from falling down the stairs. Morvina's heavy footsteps are right behind me as I pull in rushed air, forcing myself to move down the narrow steps at an uncomfortable pace.

The air feels thicker as we finally reach the bottom. A bald elf in white robes sits at a wooden table haphazardly covered in stacks of paper. He continues writing as we approach, stopping within inches of the table.

Morvina clears her throat, lifting her chin slightly.

The elf stops writing, his stone jaw and pinched eyes slowly rising to meet Morvina's stare. "Yes?" the elf asks with a slow, rocky voice that sounds rarely used.

"Marking and transport to the mines," Morvina says, dropping her portion of the chain to the floor. "I leave her in your charge. Do not remove the collar."

The elf raises an eyebrow slowly turning to look at me. His eyes widening as if just now realizing I was in the room. "Understood," he said, returning to his writing.

Without another word, Morvina begins her accent up the stairs. My breaths come easier with each step she takes.

Only when I can no longer hear her footsteps does the elf speak, "Remove your gown."

"W-what?" I stutter, taking a step back.

The elf slowly meets my eyes, my entire body becoming stiff as stone under his gaze. "Remove. Your. Gown." The temperature of the room dropping with each word.

With shaky hands I untie my gown, letting it fall to the floor. Goosebumps run along my arms as I attempt to cover myself with my arms.

The elf stands, his chair seeming to slide out from behind him on its own as he walks around the table, turning me to face away from him, "On your knees."

A sharp gasp escapes my lips as my legs touch the icy floor.

"This will hurt. Do not move, or I will need to start over. Then it will hurt more," he says, pressing his hand against my spine. "Do you understand?"

What little heat I had left drains from my face. I grit my teeth, nodding my understanding. The elf wastes no time, twisting his hand and chanting in an ancient language. I silently scream, feeling my skin twist and tear as heat slashes in patterns along my back.

I run to my mindscape, desperate for some escape. The ground splinters and quakes as I run, not knowing where to go. Flames shoot up all around me causing me to collapse, my screams echoing throughout my mind. As I fall to the ground, the pain suddenly vanishes, replaced with the sounds of birds. Moss tickles my palms as I open my eyes, pulling in large gulps of air as I take in the forest around me. I rise to my feet, enjoying the spongy feeling of the moss beneath my feet.

"Hello?" I yell, my voice unnaturally echoing off the trees.

The bushes rustle behind me as the enormous black wolf steps out. Its glowing sapphire eyes watching me. I slowly raise my hands, crouching to my knees.

"I remember you. Is this yours?" I ask, looking around as I spread my arms to either side.

The wolf narrows its eyes, tilting its head to one side.

"This... place." I say, mirroring its head tilt.

The wolf takes a step toward me, sniffing the air. I lower my head slightly, keeping my eyes glued to it as it begins to circle me. A deep thunderous growl vibrates through the air. Its lips curl up, revealing long sharp fangs.

My heart is pounding in my chest, my instincts screaming at me to run. Yet something inside me holds me back, a certainty that this wolf will not harm me. I glare at the wolf, showing my own teeth.

Its growl deepens further, lunging a few steps away from me.

I thrust my hands back, letting out my own roar, my nose inches from its snout.

The wolf steps back, lowering its head ever so slightly as its growl subsides.

"There," I sigh. "Was that so hard?" I hold my palm out to it, letting it make the next move.

It sniffs my hand, its eyes dilating to twice their size before disappearing behind its eyelids. It pushes its head into my hand. My fingers tingle, threading through its fur as it moves forward, wrapping its head over my shoulder as I take it into a hug.

Why do you feel like home?

A hand pats my back. I turn, the forest disappearing around me as I am once again in the dark room with the bald elf. My back, now throbbing with pain.

"You did well. Sleep now," the elf said. Holding a hand out to a stone slab with a thin blanket resting atop its surface.

CHAPTER 5

My tongue is stuck to the roof of my mouth, my lips cracking with warm pain as I stretch open my mouth. Thirst, it seemed, would greet me this morning in force. I look down, finding Alice's arm stretched through the bars, her hand resting on my chest. Her steady breathing and heartbeat fill my ears, telling me she is still asleep, or very relaxed. Heat radiates off of her, despite how the stone beneath us leeches every ounce of warmth it can get. Even making what remains of my tattered clothes stiff.

I can remember falling asleep as she held me, how right it felt. Yet I can't shake the feeling that something is off. Like I have been in a fog all this time and it is just now clearing.

A sliver of the morning sun peeks through a crack in the wall, caressing the stone floor just outside my cell.

I slowly adjust, lowering Alice's hand to the ground so as not to wake her. My bones ache as I rise, stretching out as much as the cramped space will allow. While the morning light isn't much, it does help me to see my surroundings better.

The man from before, he made it difficult to breathe somehow. So much so that I couldn't even think, let alone answer his questions. My head throbs as I race to recount the night. What had he asked? *Where am I from?* Why would that even matter?

I try to swallow, my tightening throat pulls my focus back to the present. *I need water.* Looking around the cell, my heartbeat increases. *They haven't left anything for us to eat, let alone drink.*

No... no... breath... I take a deep breath in through the nose, coughing as my dry throat burns. I force myself to take a much shallower breath, letting the scents of the room fill my nose. The scent of tree bark, raw meat and sweat permeate the space, but there is something else. I take another shallow breath, trying to isolate it. *Fresh, clean air? RAIN!*

My eyes are glued back to the sliver of sunlight creeping in through my cell wall. My legs shake, forcing me to brace myself against the wall to remain upright as I approach the crack. The smell of fresh morning dew and grass consumes my senses as the slightest breeze trickles in.

"What are you looking at?" Alice yawns, rubbing her eyes under strands of brown, curly hair.

"I think it might rain."

"Rain? We are underground."

I open my mouth to answer but instead snap it shut again. People back home didn't like that I was different, maybe she would think I was weird too.

"Hello? Are you still there? Why do you think it's gonna rain?" she asks, now sitting on her legs.

"The air coming in feels fresh," I said. *'Cause that sounds convincing.*

"Well, it doesn't smell great down here. So fresh air must be nice," she said with a giggle.

I rub my nose with my sleeve. She is right, it does smell of mildew and wet fur down here. *Why the wet fur?* "Yeah," I say with a forced half-laugh. "Why does everything smell like a wet dog?"

"I'm not sure." For an instant, Alice stopped scratching her head and I could hear her heart flutter. It was only an instant but it was there. "I haven't seen any dogs, how strange. Maybe that giant mutt the orc had slept in the cart with the supplies?"

My eyes pinch together, "Maybe." I look back to the crack in the wall, just as the trickling of rain hitting the ground whispers in my ear. "You hear that?"

"Wow, you must be the rain whisperer," she said. Her smile feels contagious as one stretches across my own.

I start feeling around the cell for something to use, a stone, stick, anything.

"What are you looking for?"

"Something to widen the crack."

"If they hear us, they will hurt us," Alice's voice quivered a little, drawing my gaze again.

"Did they hurt you?" My chest tightens as I ball my fists, already knowing the answer.

"No. They just... we should be careful," she says, looking to the ground.

Lie. Every muscle in my body tightens, "Alice?"

She looks toward me, keeping her eyes low. "I'm ok, let's just not make a lot of noise okay?" A gentle breeze that smells of lavender and pine flows over me, soothing my soul.

I rub my face, suddenly very aware of how tight it had gotten a moment ago. "Alright."

Alice looks up at me, her jade eyes glinting with a forced grin on her face. "I think I hear something."

I turn around, finding the slightest trickle of water flowing down the wall. I rush over, cupping my hand against the wall. The icy winter rain stings as it pools in my hand. I quickly drink every small amount I can, feeling the relief as the moisture puts out the fire in my throat. "Do you want some?" I ask, gathering more water in my hands.

"Please," she pleads, licking her lips.

I rush over to her, small droplets of water escaping between my fingers. "It's cold," I said, pouring the water into her hands. She drinks it instantly, some flowing down her cheek and dripping onto her tunic. Her hardened nipples pushing against the thin fabric.

"Eyes up here Alex," Alice chides with a grin.

"I... I was..." I stutter, feeling my cheeks heat. "Let me get you more water."

Alice and I had spent what felt like hours in an awkward silence, listening to the sounds of the morning rain subside. My skin was crawling, the cell itself, shrinking in around me.

I need to get out of here.

"Soooo, what happened to your back?" Alice asks, her words echoing off the walls.

Why is she being so loud? Wasn't it her idea to stay quiet? Maybe she was quiet... I was trying to hear anything from outside this cave after all. "What?" I ask, finally realizing she had asked me a question.

"You have scars on your back, what happened?"

I pull what's left of my shirt tighter around me. "Wolves attacked me when I was a kid. I don't remember much of what happened," I say, turning my face toward the faint light still trickling in through that single crack in the wall.

I hear her pants drag along the floor as she scoots closer to the bars that separate us. "It's nothing to be ashamed of. I've got some too, see?"

When I turn, she has her sleeve pulled up to her elbow, revealing a bite-sized scarred patch of skin on her forearm that is paler than the skin around it. "I got this one a few years ago." Her eyes linger on the scar for a few moments, a smile tugging at the corners of her mouth. "Do you know what type of wolf it was?"

"I'm not sure, I was with..." Footsteps echo off the walls from the doorway. I take a deep breath, centering my focus back to the here and now. Noticing how Alice has already shuffled to the opposite side of her cell, as if trying to conceal herself in the farthest shadows.

The scent of sweat and dirt wafts into the cell, the burly man from before entering with his fists curled. He stops before my cell, his focus lingering on Alice before finally coming to rest on me. The air in the room instantly becomes heavier the moment our eyes lock. I feel my chest tighten, as we continue our stair down. My head begins to throb as I look to the floor, finally able to take a breath.

"Good, at least you know your place. Now, *where* are you from?" the man asks.

I feel the veins popping out of my neck as I fight my instinct, trying desperately to meet his gaze again. Only making it to his boots that I note have the same amount of mud on them. "Why does it matter?" I ask through gritted teeth.

"I am the one asking the questions. Now tell me, where are you from?"

My elbows buckle but remain steady, sweat building on my forehead. It feels like the entire cave has collapsed onto my back and I am fighting for my life. "No."

"No?" the man asks, his boot dragging backwards slightly. "I had hoped spending some time with Alice would help. I don't like pushing new blood so soon. It just makes everything else harder, but I won't have you telling me *no*." The last word came out in a growl. His calloused hands grip my chin through the bars, pulling my eyes to meet his. My own widen, filling with fear as I notice that they have shifted from a gentle brown to a vibrant yellow. "Now, I'm not asking. Tell me where you are from."

My mouth opens on its own, words forming on their own, "I'm..." *NO!* "From..." My own screams crash through my mind. My lungs threaten to burst as his gaze burns through me, "Red River." The moment the words leave my lips he releases my chin and my entire body collapses to the ground as I fight for air.

"*Get up,*" a low growling voice full of rage sounds through my mind.

Everything begins to take on a blue hue. My teeth are grinding as my jaw protests under the pressure. *What is happening?*

I can barely hear muffled words, unable to make them out or tell who said them. My muscles begin to swell, as if twisting and stretching on their own. Every one of my nerves are on fire as I scream out, no longer recognizing the sound of my own voice.

"Shit! No, no, no, not yet, come back to me," Alice's gentle voice caresses my ear, her arms wrapping around me.

My nose fills with the smell of fresh river water and spring flowers that remind me of home. The place I had been ripped away from. My muscles continue to twist, an audible pop filling my ears as another scream erupts from my throat.

Alice squeezes her arms tighter, the air around me crackling with power. "It's ok," she coos, moving her lips inches from my ear. "You're safe now." She pets my hair slowly. The smell of home wrapping around me, overpowering all other senses, my eyes growing heavy. "I have you. You're safe. Just breathe."

The blue hues dim, my muscles settle into a numb ache. "What?" My question falls short, feeling the world slip away.

As I open my eyes again, I am running low to the ground through a forest. The brush flowing past me in blurs of green and orange. My mind feels heavy, almost foggy. My entire body moving on its own, as if I were merely a passenger. The crisp night air fills my lungs, the soft soil under my feet. I hear crickets singing as I pass.

I feel free.

How did I get here?

I suddenly come to stop, looking all around. Only the sounds of the forest surround me. I can faintly make out the sound of a fawn grazing a few yards away. It feels strange, my muscles moving in ways they never have before as I creep forward on all fours.

The fawn comes into view. It is facing away from me, grazing on some briars. My heartbeat increases, my mouth watering as my tongue impossibly licks my nose. It is completely unaware that I am so close. I take another step forward, the fawn's ears shoot up, looking off to the right. My eyes follow its gaze then snap back to the fawn who has begun sprinting away.

"Hello?" a faint female voice shouts through the forest.

My bones feel like shattered glass. Alice is humming a soothing tune while petting my head. Dried sweat clings to my skin as I peer up at her, realizing that my head is resting in her lap.

I push past the pain, clearing the last bit of morning blur from my vision.

Shock jolts through my body as I realize, *I'm not resting against the bars.* I look up, and meet Alice's eyes again.

"Welcome back. You will still be a bit raw, so take it slow," her voice is gentle and warm as her hands move down to my shoulders.

"What happened?" I ask, my throat hoarse, as though I had been screaming for hours.

"You were changing, it was violent though. Like you were fighting it."

"Changing?" The confusion on my face quickly reflected in hers.

"Have... have you... Alex, when did you get those scars?" Alice asked, her eyebrows pinching together.

"When I was six... why?"

"And you've been drinking Nitpaw since then?"

"I think so, why?"

Alice's face pales, her mouth slightly open as she stares through me. Her obvious concern was only amplified by the fact that her skin was cold to the touch.

"Alice? Are you okay?"

She shakes her head, a genuine smile spouting on her face as a tear flows down her cheek. In that moment I realized, the other smiles she had worn, the subtle smirks, they hadn't been real. She had been wearing a mask, just like the one I wore for Altha.

"We have a lot to talk about," she says, wiping her nose with her sleeve. "I... we are not human."

My eyebrow rises, "Then what are you?"

"Well, we *are* human, but we are also werewolves."

Werewolves? Altha had told me stories about them while I was growing up. How they would sneak into villages in the dead of night, murdering and stealing people away. But they were just that, children's stories to make you behave. "You're... *werewolves?*"

"Yes, and so are you."

I give a half-hearted laugh, but Alice doesn't join in, her face remaining straight. "You're serious?" I wait, but she just continues to stare at me. "Werewolves transform into, well, wolves during the full moon. Everyone has heard those stories."

"Those stories are incorrect, mostly. Newly turned werewolves, ones that have not yet taken their first change, do so on their first Full Moon. This is the time when we are best connected with our wolf and thus at our strongest. So yes, many werewolves will shift during the Full Moon but only new werewolves *have* to."

"But you said I am a werewolf... I'm pretty sure I would remember turning into a wolf even once."

"You haven't." The words appearing to bring her physical discomfort. "Nitpaw is toxic to werewolves. It can weaken, even suppress a bond between human and wolf. Since you have been taking it so long it built up in your system, suppressing your wolf."

"I take Nitpaw for…" The words dying on my tongue as embarrassment overshadows my confidence.

Alice let out a shallow laugh, "Let me guess. Before you take it, you feel your heart pounding in your chest, like the world is getting too loud around you. That everything is getting too close. That you are going to be swallowed up?"

I bit at the inside of my mouth, unsure what to say other than *yes*.

"Yeah, I'm sure that's what whoever gave it to you said it was for," she said, spitting on the ground.

"She wouldn't lie to me," I said. Pushing up and walking to the opposite end of the cell, the tension in my chest builds with each step.

Alice gives me a sympathetic look, "They never do."

"She wouldn't!" I shout, my vision flashing blue for an instant, causing me to stumble back.

Alice throws up her hands, "Alright, alright. I don't want a fight. You take a minute. I'm going to be outside when you're ready to talk," she says, pushing open the cell door with a single finger and walking out into the passage without another word.

Memories of Altha telling me not to comment on what I smelled or overhead flash through my mind. The countless times she drilled into my head the exact proportions for the Nitpaw brew. Ensuring that I never ran out of it through the winter months. How she had stopped hosting knowledge sharing days at home and opted for mail correspondence instead.

The letter.

I reach into my pocket, and there it is. Still sealed. Addressed to Altha from an Irithiel. Without thinking I tear the seal, pulling out the small piece of parchment.

Altha,

I appreciate your kind words for the passing of my late husband. Toward the end it was invaluable to have the mixture you provided for Nettleryn. Just as you said, three drops in his tea at night allowed him to pass peacefully. Simply falling asleep for the final time.

As for your boy, I am very sorry to hear of the heightened immunity to the Nitpaw brew. I would remind you however, that the Elders warned that this course of action was foolish.

They told you that it was never meant to keep the demon from taking root, only to grant the human a moment of clarity without the influence of the demon within them.

Finally, I would remind you that you made that deal all those years ago for a reason. I know you have tried your hardest to care for the boy. I am sure she would have been proud of you as well. With that in mind, you know what you must do. The time has come.

May the sun guide your path.

,Irithiel

The air feels like ice, time itself standing still as I hold the parchment in shaky hands. My tears soaking into it. "She wouldn't..."

The sound of familiar humming breaks the eerie silence that I have been sitting in for long enough that my knees ache. I look at the letter intended for Altha, damp and crumpled in my hands. My heart feels empty as I rise, shoving the paper into my pocket.

The humming floats along the walls. I pass several caved-in sections, finally reaching the moss-covered stairs at the end of the passage.

As I ascend the stairs, the overwhelming smell of mildew and wet fur is replaced by the smell of wet pine. I find Alice leaning against a boulder. Her eyes closed with both her arms and legs crossed as she continues to hum the seemingly never-ending tune.

I stare out along the dirt road that Sarfu had brought us in on. Deep gouges from where his heavy carts had been resting are still shown on its surface.

"You should know that you wouldn't make it very far if you tried to run. Richard keeps a constant perimeter patrol on rotation that would catch your scent before you even made it out of the woods," Alice announces with a bitter tone.

I feel a bubbling heat course through my blood. All of my muscles tighten as I throw my arms out. "Why the games? Why lock me up down there with you? Why let me out at all?"

She barely opens her eyes to look at me, the jade of her eyes glowing.

"And why do your eyes glow? I saw the other guys do that too."

"It happens when the wolf is close to the surface. As for your other questions, we did it to give you time."

"What?" I spit out, my eyebrows tightening.

"When you got here you reeked of Nitpaw. You had so much in your system you were practically sweating it out. Then the orc told Marcus all about your scars and how fast you heal. That was enough for us to know that you were a werewolf. So, Marcus decided that you needed time to get that shit out of your system, and we needed time to figure out how many of you there were. As for why you were with me? I'm the Omega of the pack, I make it easier for out-of-control *pups* to keep control of themselves. Without me, Richard probably would have killed you down there," she says, her nose wrinkling as she said Richard's name.

The taste of iron fills my mouth, my chest rising with each breath as I take a step back. *How many of me there were?* My eyes widen in realization, "You're going to Red River."

She took a moment, looking me up and down, "Before I answer that, take a few deep breaths."

Why? Don't like my attitude toward being locked up and lied to? I take several deep breaths, feeling my blood cool with each one. Knowing that she is right, I wouldn't make it out on my own. *Yet.*

"Thank you. Richard took three wolves out to check if you were the only one. Based on how you've been acting, I'm going to guess you are."

"Are they... going to hurt anyone?"

"You can ask when they get back tonight," she said, pushing off the boulder. "Follow me, unless you aren't hungry."

I look down the path and then back to her as my stomach makes a truly awful rumbling sound. "So, who is Richard?" I ask, following Alice along the side of the mansion.

"He is the Beta of the pack."

"And... what is that?" I ask, my eyes lingering on a shattered window that had been boarded up.

"The second in command to the Alpha, they lead the hunts and ensure everyone stays in line. You could say that they are the muscle of the pack," she said. She opens a short rusty gate, its sound making me grind my teeth.

"Does that make him stronger than the Alpha?" I ask, quickly pushing the gate shut with a *clang*.

Alice chuckles, rounding the corner. "Definitely not, but don't tell him that. Anything we can do to help?"

At least ten large, worn oak tables are scattered around the yard. A young woman with short brown hair stands in its center stacking various sizes of wood in an enormous raised fire pit that forms a cross. She is roughly the same height as Alice, with soothing blue eyes.

"Hey Alice, if you could help with the racks that would be great. This him?" she inquires, with a nod in my direction.

"Yeah, this is Alex. Alex, this is Mia. I'll go get those racks, why don't you help Mia fill the pit?" She said, walking toward the house before I could answer.

"You don't smell like a wolf, but at least you don't smell like that awful brew anymore," Mia said, turning to continue stacking wood.

"Thanks?" I say, smelling myself with a sneeze. *Mildew... I smell like mildew.* "How long have you been a werewolf?" I ask, sliding a log into the pit.

"I'm not sure." She looked to the moon, a smile growing across her face as she closed her eyes. "At least forty years."

My eyes narrow, she can't be over twenty-two. I let out a shallow laugh, "What's your secret?"

Her body went stiff, "I... I'm..." The wood in her hand creaking under her white-knuckle grip.

A gentle breeze sweeps past us, the leaves kicking up the scent of pine barely holding on against the winter freeze. "Werewolves don't age after their first shift," Alice states, holding several long, thin sheets of charred tin with hundreds of holes through them. I look back to Mia, her shoulders lower again as she smiles at Alice.

"Yeah, sorry. I was turned right before my twenty-first winter. Time has felt weird since then," her voice, stuttering at first, had taken on a calm, centered focus.

"Are you ok?" I ask, reaching out my hand, choosing to ignore the relaxing energy that radiates from Alice and instead focus on the tension that had just surrounded Mia.

"Fine," she snaps, looking at me with yellow eyes that scream *stay away*.

The image of her growing huge fangs and biting my hand clean off flash thought my mind. Causing me to snatch my hand back. "Alright, just making sure."

"Alex, could you please help me with these sheets? The hunting party should be back soon."

CHAPTER 6

Awkward silence shrouds the backyard as Alice and I tie venison to sticks. Mia, now converting a small stick into a makeshift torch, is laughing with a little girl that had come out of the mansion.

She appears to be roughly six years old with black hair and a button nose. The urge to go over and apologize for whatever I had done to upset Mia is eating at me. While another part of me is terrified that she might make those earlier images a reality.

"It's not polite to stare," Alice said, flicking my ear.

"She seems different with her. Like she is a different person," I said, finally getting the string to wrap around the venison and the stick at the same time.

"She *is* a completely different person."

I rub my forehead, cringing at the slime from the venison that lingers there. "Do I need to ask?"

"Only if you want the answer," she said with a grin.

I let out a sigh, pressing the back of my hands against my eyes, "Okay, what do you mean she is a completely different person?"

"I'm so glad you asked. Mia's wolf took over, my guess is she was having a hard time with your energy."

"Mia's wolf? So that isn't Mia right now?"

"Well, it is, and it isn't. She is still present, watching what is happening but her wolf is calling the shots."

"So, was I upsetting Mia, or her wolf?"

"Both probably," Alice said with a chuckle. "Mia is a submissive in the pack but her wolf is dominant. *Most* dominants have a hard time when someone is making their submissives feel small. You experienced that down in the cell with Richard."

My eyes widen, looking between Mia and Alice, "I was making her feel that?"

"Probably nothing like what Richard was making you feel down there. Then again, maybe you did. I am not getting a good enough read on your energy. You did have a lot of Nitpaw built up, you have felt... strange these last few nights."

"Wouldn't you have felt if I was dominant?"

"Nope. Each wolf has different abilities that they may or may not choose to share with their partner. My wolf shares her ability to sooth the spirits of others. Dominants have a hard time dominating when you make them big fluff balls."

"Wait, the scents, that's you?"

"Is that what it does for you? It's different for everyone," Alice said, tossing her fifth perfectly tied off bundle of meat onto one of the tin sheets.

My focus drifts down to the ruined pieces of meat in my hands, wondering how I am going to get this to tie off at this point. "You make this look easy," I say in defeat. The little girl rushes over, whispering into Alice's ear. Mia's yellow eyes track her every step with a loving grin.

Alice pulls her into a hug, causing her to burst into a giggling fit before Alice whispers something back into her ear. She then lifts her to her feet, kissing her forehead and sending her skipping back to Mia's lap.

"Children are precious, a reminder of how truly fragile life can be. Even for us," Alice said, her gaze lingering on the little girl.

"Is she a...?"

"Yes and no. It's not common for werewolves to conceive, even rarer that the baby survives through birth. Born werewolves don't take their first full moon change until their eighteen, which is good because it is extremely hard on the body," she says, the moonlight caressing her face. "Now scoot, let's see if we can salvage your disaster."

The intoxicating smell of the burning logs and sound of the sizzling meat had my mouth watering as I imagined how juicy a single bite would be. The majority of the hunting party has returned. Each carrying a deer on their shoulders, each one larger than the last. I guess even werewolves have the "*mines bigger*" mentality.

"Stop daydreaming and flip the meat," Alice scolds.

"Sorry," I say, quickly turning over several sticks. Some of the meat was a little burnt, but my stomach still assured me that they would be delicious.

"I'll be right back, try not to burn down the forest while I'm gone."

"No promises," I say, observing the small groups scattered around the yard. Some are swapping stories about the hunt, some taking a nap, some... *moon bathing*? Mia's daughter is eating more food off her mom's plate than her own, followed shortly by a giggle every time her mom snatches a bite from hers.

I flip the meat again, looking up to spot Alice having an intense conversation with Marcus at a table all their own from the looks of it. At least on Alice's side it looked intense, talking more with her arms and facial expressions than anything else. Marcus has his chair leaned back on two legs with his ankles crossed over each other on the table.

Feeling that the meat was cooked enough, I pull the last few sticks off the sheet, untying the different bundles and adding them onto the heaping pile on the center table.

Knowing that my eyes are probably bigger than my stomach, I choose to grab two chunks for myself, jogging over to a tree where we hung what's left of the hunter's catches. The stench of decay is much more appealing than trying to mingle on an empty stomach.

My legs throb with appreciation as I take my seat, closing my eyes. I imagine an elegant deer in my mind, standing in front of me deep within the forests. *Thank you, because of you I may continue to live.* I take my first bite without opening my eyes. Savoring the smooth, rich flavors accented by a hint of pine and berries. An overpowering sense of joy washes over me for the first time since leaving home.

"Chose to sit alone, huh?," Alice muses, leaning against the tree. I can't help the confusion that washes over my face as I note that she is precariously holding *five* chunks of meat. "My butt hurts from sitting on the cell floor these last few days, but I also don't like eating alone. Would you mind joining me at that table?"

My eyes follow her nod to a small empty table near the edge of the yard. *It's not in the center at least...* "Sure." I grit my teeth as pain burns through my legs. Their not-so-subtle reminder that I only just sat down.

Oddly enough I feel like I have less eyes on me as I walk beside Alice. Despite the people pointing and whispering from tables we pass on the way. Confusion clouds my mind as I hear their whispers but can't make out what they said.

"Why can't I make out what they are whispering?" I ask Alice once we sit down.

"Why so nosey?" Alice asks with a raised eyebrow. "You think they are talking about how the new pup is walking around with their precious Omega?"

The table could maybe seat four people, if they squeezed in real close. No wonder people had left this table empty.

More like how are they going to get me away from their Omega.

"Yeah," I mumble back, shifting uneasily.

"Pack magic has a tendency to protect the privacy of its members. No one really understands why or how, just that when you would prefer not to be heard you typically won't be," she said, tearing into her first chuck of venison with vigor.

I feel every hair on my neck stand straight up, causing me to freeze mid bite. "I see you got the pup out from the hole," a deep, raspy voice said from directly behind me.

My eyes widen, watching Alice for some sign that I was okay. *I should have stayed by the tree.*

Alice shrugged her shoulders, continuing to chew through a rather large bite that barely fit in her mouth, "He walked out on his own."

Richard rounded the table, his hand resting on the nap of Alice's neck as he took his seat. A young, scrawny man rushes over a moment later, sliding a plate piled high with meat in front of him before scurrying back to wherever he had come from. "Now, now, we talked about that. Swallow, then respond," his yellow teeth shining through his grin.

Alice's eyes cracked open, revealing her shimmering jade eyes. A bead of sweat rolls down my back as she watches me.

"I'm," I get out before Richard's head snaps to me.

His eyes flashing yellow for the faintest of seconds. "Keep eating pup," he commands, moving Alice's hair to one side. He leans in burying his face into her neck, "You smell nice."

Alice's teeth grind together as she tilts her head away. Swallowing hard enough that I could hear the gulp from across the table, "I thought we agreed not to do this in the open."

"What's the difference, they all know. Besides, you didn't keep up your end of that little agreement."

"Marcus told me to ensure the boy didn't hurt himself. You know how badly we need new blood, especially after your stupid stunt."

Richard rips a small chunk of meat free, sucking the tips of his fingers clean after the bite. "You aren't going to hurt yourself, are you, boy?"

I feel the weight of the world pressing down on my shoulders, unable to form words as I shake my head. I feel the invisible force subside, instantly replaced by the sound of my own heart racing, my muscles tightening with anticipation.

"See? Marcus will be thrilled. Now come with me," he says, reaching for Alice's hand.

Alice shifts her weight to the side, slapping his hand away, "I'm eating."

Richard's confident grin turns sour as he jolts to his feet. The entire table shifts as he reaches out, taking a fist full of Alice's hair into his hand," I said.

I feel my hands tighten, a crack echoing through the yard. I look down, shock shooting through me. At some point I had gone from holding food to gripping the table and now my fingertips were buried deep into one of the boards.

Richard's brown eyes look to me, "You have something to say pup?"

I fight the urge to look away, keeping my eyes locked with his. "She said she was eating," I reply through gritted teeth.

"Oh? You hear that, the pup doesn't think you want to come with me," he says, pulling her head closer.

What am I doing? He is massive. Each of my breaths bursting out of my lungs, requiring more effort with each passing second.

Richard let out a deep laugh, looking out at the others around us, "I thought you knew your place. We should correct that immediately," he says, releasing Alice's hair with a shove.

"Richard don't," Alice said, rubbing her head.

"No, no, I can't leave a challenge unanswered. You know that," Richard says, gripping my arm and pulling me to the center of the yard, several people moving their tables to create a small open space.

My eyes dart back to Alice, still sitting at the table. Everyone else has stopped eating, watching with their eyes low.

"Since you're new I'll explain. We are going to fight, until either one of us submits to the other, or is unable to continue. Make sense?"

I nod my head, flexing my hands to relieve some nerves.

"Good, try to make this fun," he snarks, cracking his knuckles. "I will let you have a free shot."

I feel my entire face tighten as I throw my entire weight behind my fist, slamming into his chest.

He doesn't budge an inch as I feel my arm vibrating from the impact. A smile creeps across his face, "My turn."

I blink, feeling a hand slap across my face, throwing me to the ground. Blood pools in my mouth as I struggle to rise, seeing stars on the edge of my vision. A hand grips my hair, jerking me to my feet.

"You are weak!" he growled, punching me hard in the back. "You are here only if I allow it." Another punch to the back that sends shocks down to my feet as I fall to my knees. "You are beneath me." His arm locks around my throat, "You will *always* be beneath me."

My vision becomes blurry. Alice looks across the yard at me, pity written across her face.

Don't pity me! A growl echoes through my mind. My blurry vision fading into a blue hue. I feel fire push out through my arm as it shoots up, my fingers digging into Richard's nose, pulling forward hard as I turn my face, ripping into his arm with my teeth.

Richard roars, loosening his hold just enough for me to plant my feet, kicking off the ground and slamming him into a table with a *crunch!*

Finally free I tumble forward. The blue hues fading away, along with my sudden surge of strength, leaving me panting for air as I look back to Richard.

He laughs, dabbing the blood trailing from his nose and lips as his now yellow eyes lock on me, "Lucky shot." He spits blood to the side. He lurches forward is fist cracking against my skull, sending me into the dirt.

Pain pulses through my head as I jolt up, throwing my arms up to block the next punch. But it never comes. Panting, I slowly lower my hands, looking from side to side.

I am laying on a torn-up bedroll that has been spread across a battered bed frame. The room has peeling wallpaper and a window with a hazy buildup. I pull myself to my feet, gasping as searing white pain ripples out from my ribs. Muffled conversation brings my focus to the only door leading out of the room.

The copper knob turns in my hand, the door screeching as it opens freely. *So much for being quiet.*

"Afternoon sunshine! If you want any semblance of a meal, I recommend getting down here quickly," Marcus' voice called from down the hall.

An orange light from the wall sconces illuminates the hallway, highlighting the specks of the original polished floor along the baseboards while the majority of its surface is worn to the bare wood. It would remind me of George's trade house, if his trade house hadn't been cleaned for several decades.

Not knowing exactly where Marcus' voice had originated from, I choose to follow the sound of clattering silverware which brings me to the relatively clean dining room. Marcus is seated at the end of a large table that could seat at least twelve people. A large log fire burning in the stone fireplace behind him. Above it rests an enormous empty frame that is hanging at an angle.

"Come, sit," Marcus says, pointing with his fork to the chair beside him.

My steps echo off the walls as I approach, making me feel even more uneasy about being alone with, presumably, the Alpha of the werewolves. *Alice said the Alpha was strong, right?*

The smell of brown sugar and honey fill the room as Marcus cuts into a slab of light gray meat with practiced hands. His leather jacket is draped over the back of his chair, revealing his scarred, muscular body. He carefully places each bite into his mouth, dabbing his lips right after even though it had clearly never touched his lips. "You made my second quite displeased, challenging him in front of the Pack like that."

I slide into my chair, its soft red cushions feel like riding a sheep, just without the itchy part, "I wasn't challenging him."

Marcus stops chewing, looking at me for a moment with a raised eyebrow before continuing to finish his bite. "Interesting. He says quite the opposite," he remarks, snapping his fingers and pointing in front of me.

A slim, young boy, maybe fifteen, rushes over, laying a similar plate to what Marcus has in front of me before vanishing back to wherever he had materialized from. Within seconds, the invigorating scent of butter, honey and salt fills my nose. "Alice wanted him to leave her alone. He was the one getting aggressive."

Marcus' eyes shimmer amber for a second before returning to their human teal, "Richard has been with me from the beginning, and has earned his place. You are a new pup that was denied the truth of your existence. For this, I have prevented Richard from exacting his right to kill you for challenging him. Know that I will not prevent it again. Should you defy him further, it will be within his right. He is your Beta now, whether you want it or not. Lone wolves are not allowed in my territory."

"I *am* a prisoner then," I bite out with a more aggressive tone than I had intended.

The air in the room becomes heavy, an invisible force pinning my hands to the table. I look at Marcus, his eyes still a gentle teal, yet his glare threatens to tear me in half. "I have been patient with your arrival. I can use the additional blood in the Pack, but you will learn your place here. Show the proper respect, or I will banish you to the woods and let the Pack hunt you down."

I lower my gaze, the truth of his words sending a shiver to my core. *Breath...*

Marcus turns his gaze back to his plate as the air becomes normal again. I rub my wrists, feeling the blood return to them.

"Now please, eat. Tonight is the full moon and you will need strength."

I walk the halls of the mansion before finally finding the door to the backyard. The orange beams of the evening sun warm my skin as I take in the tables that had been full the night before. Mia and her starry-eyed daughter are the only two out here, but still making the space feel full. The table they are at has an already skinned deer that they are in the process of carving.

"Remember to cut away, always cut away," Alice says, her yellow eyes peering over her shoulder at me.

I can feel the sweat building on my palms as I approach. "Heyyyy... I don't mean to interrupt. I just wanted to apologize. For the other day."

Mia turns to face me, wiping her blood covered hands on her brown tunic. The image of her biting my hand clean off replaying in my mind.

"I didn't mean to come off... dominantly? I'm still figuring this out," I said, feeling a little stupid.

Lue peeks out from behind Mia. Bursting into a run as she tackles into my leg hard enough that I have to brace with my other foot to not fall.

"It's ok," she said looking back at Mia as she continued to hug my leg with her blood-soaked arms. "Right mommy? He didn't mean it."

My hands are floating to either side, every instinct telling me that momma wolf might kill me if I even think about touching baby wolf.

Mia tilts her head to one side, squinting as she watches me. "You're right Lue, it's important to forgive mistakes," Mia says, half turning back to the carcass they had been working on. "We understand."

"I see you two are getting along," Alice observes from directly behind me, grabbing my arm. "I need to steal Alex away for a bit Lue, you be good for mommy, okay?"

"Ok. Bye!" Lue calls out, bouncing back to Mia's side.

"You need to teach me how to be that quiet," I say as Alice pulls me along the path beside the mansion.

"Nothing to teach, pack magic does what it wants when it wants," Alice snaps, her movements stiff. "You need to be more careful. What you did last night was stupid."

I come to an abrupt stop, twisting my arm out of her grasp. My brows pinch together, "Excuse me?"

"Richard has been a full werewolf for sixty plus years. On top of that he is the Beta of the Pack. You haven't even been a werewolf for a single day and you choose to fight him? For what? You think you have some claim on me?"

I can feel my blood beginning to boil as I take a long deep breath, choosing to let silence sit between us rather than answer the question.

"There's nothing between us, okay? I was down there because Marcus wanted me down there. I have been helping you because Marcus wants me to."

Breath... One... Two...

"What? Did I hit a nerve? You having a hard time holding yourself together without me helping push all that pent up rage down?"

Thh.... three... four... The fifth deep breath I pull in through my nose, instantly overcome by the scent of soap, like someone had washed themselves eight times. Yet the faintest smell hid behind it all. It feels like dumping a bucket of ice water over the top of my head, "You slept with him?" I ask.

Shame flashes across her face, disappearing into fury, amplified even more by her now shimmering jade eyes, "It's none of your business what I do!"

Silence fills the void between us, only broken up by the sound of our breathing. It's so quiet that I can hear Mia hush Lue who had mumbled something.

"It's not like that, you deserve better than..."

"I *deserve* to not be surrounded by idiot boys pretending to be men." There is a rumbling growl behind her words. She closes her eyes, taking several steps back, each with a deep breath. When she opens them again, the shimmer is gone. "Marcus wants you in the cave. You will be joined by two other wolves for the full moon. I won't be there. I make it hard for dominants to be stupid after all," she says, starting to walk away. "Last piece of advice, Richard chose them, so watch out. You're not pack until your wolf establishes his place among us."

CHAPTER 7

My bones feel like glass as I slam against the wooden floor of the cart. My large orc escort, dressed in studded leathers, latching the door closed. Thick metal bars are the only barrier between me and the frigid mid-day air. I rub my bare arms, biting my lip as I hold back tears.

The cart lurches forward, pulling us out of the stable and out to the quiet streets. High Elves and their servants watch, their eyes filled with fury and disgust.

"Traitor!" someone in the crowd screams just before a brick slams against the bars.

I shuffle back on all fours, slamming against the opposite side of the cart.

"Witch!" another screams, the bars directly behind my head rattling from another impact.

"No!" I cry out, scrambling back to the center of the cart.

"Monster!" Bits of rotting food fly through bars, slamming against me.

I bury my head between my knees, rocking back and forth with the cart as it bounces against the stone street. Desperate to drown out the crowd's slurs. I want to go back to the night Morvina told us of the escort task and beg to have someone, anyone else go. To wake up and believe this was all just a bad dream.

Something sharp slices along my arm as I grip even harder, tears flowing down my cheeks as the crowds shouting becomes deafening. *I'm not... I'm not... I'm not...*

The sound of the roaring crowd suddenly gasping makes my eyes shoot up, taking in four shadow guards. Their spears drawn, now blocking the crowd's advance. *Why? Why would they protect me?* I look around, my hand slamming over my mouth, a silent scream tearing through my chest as I feel my heart explode. Rivers of tears flood down my face.

Iromae was right, she had not been forgiven. Her limp body hangs from a pillar, the rope tight around her neck. Thousands of cuts and fresh bruises cover her exposed flesh. The small fragments of cloth that cling to her skin are caked in blood.

It's all my fault... I'm so sorry...

The inner gates creak, ushering us forward. Crowds once again line the streets, but instead of screams we are met with silence. Their eyes are filled not with fear or hatred, but sadness and pity.

My hollow bones rattle as I tremble, fearing the inevitable slur to be shouted that will ignite the crowd once more.

Instead, an old orc, covered in soot, slowly pulls his hat down, gripping it tight against his chest. Others around him follow suit.

The guards in shimmering armor, unmoving within the crowd before, turn marching towards them. They shove them to their knees.

"Liars!" someone in the crowd yells, a rock flying through the air, not at me but the driver of the cart.

"Get back!" the guards yell in unison, drawing their swords.

The driver ducks his head narrowly avoiding another stone as he cracks the reins, sending the horses into a gallop. I uncontrollably tumble into the bars, watching as we leave the screaming crowd behind.

The air tastes of ash as we enter the Nightstone Mines just outside the walls of Everenthia. Plumes of black smoke billow out of the giant central chasm. Coming to a stop near the pit, I continue to look around in confusion. A narrow bridge carved out of the gray stone leads to the center of the pit, where a single wooden structure stands. A seemingly endless shaft of wood jutting down into the abyss. *No guards?*

The orc unlatches the barred door, grunting as he gestures with his head for me to get out.

The wet, jagged stones stab into my bare feet as I climb out of the cart. Feeling the soot cling to me with each step as we make our way across the bridge.

Enormous chains dangle along the wooden shaft deep into the pitch black caves below us, the smoke rising up to greet us is my only assurance that there must be a bottom. I suddenly stop, feeling a strange heat envelope my toes. I try to pull it back but feel a tug, as if my foot is stuck in thick mud. I pull harder with no avail, my momentum shifting forward as I feel the warmth travel up my leg. The orc shoves me forward, the heat washing over my entire body.

I spin, looking at him with wide eyes, "What was that?"

He smiles, stepping to the side and raising his arm towards the cart with a raised brow.

Confusion shifts through my mind as I take the first step, "You're letting me go?"

A feral grin grows on his face, revealing his shaved tusks.

I push off hard, sprinting forward. If he is going to let me run, I am not questioning it. Joy fills my heart as I look back, the orc still smiling with his arms crossed over his chest. *He really is letting me go.* I turn, the end of the bridge just in view before something hard hits my hand, and then my face. Sending me slamming onto my back, gasping for air.

I look around for what hit me, seeing nothing.

Bellowing laughter erupts from the orc. An ear-to-ear smile plastered across his face as he watches me struggle to my feet.

I lift my hand, slowly moving it forward as it presses against solid air. Heat pulses over my back in waves. *The tattoo...* I make a fist, slamming it against the invisible barrier. *No guards...* I fight back the tears welling in my eyes. *Stay strong, she would be strong.*

My heart is pounding in my chest as I turn, walking back down the path with a confidence I do not feel, shooting daggers with my eyes at the orc as I pass.

The orc grunts a laugh, following behind me.

I pull the short wooden gate aside, the entire bathroom sized room bouncing as I enter, forcing me to cling to the walls.

He shuts the gate, latching it from the outside, pointing his finger at me. "Stay still," he commands, before rotating a wooden crank.

The entire room begins to descend, my stomach sinking with it. This was why there were no guards, one way in, one way out. I stare at the cloud covered sky, desperate for any light that I could be gifted as I descend into darkness.

After several minutes it becomes difficult to make out the wooden structure from above. The sound of crashing metal against stone echoes along the walls. The occasional scream from below sends a shiver down my spine. The sound reminding me of the pain Iromae must have experienced before being granted death. I cover my mouth, trying to filter out the thick smoke that is continually burning my throat.

"Elevator! Elevator!" several voices shout from down below.

I slowly peak over the edge. My heart leaps from my chest as the entire cage-like room shifts with my step. I gasp for air, white knuckles gripping the wooden frame as I take in the small keep that I am descending into the center of. A single bridge leads out from it over a large moat. The spikes filling the moat are discolored, some skewering the skeletal remains of several races. Archers are positioned along the battlements, their bows casually at their sides as they watch my cage descend.

Two High Elf guards approach. They pull open the gate with cruel smiles across their faces, "You think the Warden will take this one?" one of them asks with a laugh.

"I would if I was him," the other says, pulling me out of the cage by my arm.

"Maybe he is still asleep? We could..."

"Is everything in order?" a deep scratchy voice asks from behind them.

They both scramble to stand at attention, "Yes, Warden," they reply in unison.

The Warden is a High Elf as well. Displeasure is written across his plump face, one of his sausage hands resting on his round stomach that hangs over his belt. His thin white hair slicked back, glistening as if he had just splashed it with water.

"My dear, let's get you into some new attire before assigning you to your tunnel. I will explain how things work down here while we do so." His words are gentle, but I can't shake the sinking feeling in my stomach. He glances at both the guards, "Dismissed."

The Warden led me to a small room, filled with cubbies, each one labeled with unique markings beneath them.

"Stand there," he said, pointing to the wall. Hundreds of lines had been carved into its surface with the corresponding markings to the cubbies.

"I haven't had a worker with a nullification collar in a while. Just in case you get any ideas, removing the collar incorrectly will kill you. So, leave it alone."

My trembling fingers graze the soft leather, having forgotten it was there.

His stiff hand rests on the top of my head as he looks at the wall behind me. "You're short for an elf," the Warden remarks, reaching for a set of clothes.

"I'm *half* elf."

"Aside from your height, you hide it well. You will find people down here more accepting of that," he says, handing me the set of rough, thin, orange clothes with a pair of black ankle high fabric shoes. "Now get dressed."

I look around for a room, shifting uneasily between my feet.

"I said get changed girl, not appreciate the decor."

I start with my pants first. Pulling them up under my tattered robes. I can feel his eyes watching my every move, hearing his labored breaths increase in speed.

"While living within my mine, you will work to earn the privilege of clean clothes and food. Every day, five minutes after you hear the bell you must arrive at the pavilion just across the bridge. We do not feed every tunnel at the same time so listen for the bell within *your* assigned tunnel. If you come to another tunnel's meal time, or you are late for your tunnel's meal time, you will forfeit your meal for the day. If you arrive without anything to trade, you will forfeit your meal for the day."

He paused, biting his lip as I pulled the shirt over my dress, wiggling my arms to slide them out of the robe's sleeves and into the shirt's sleeves.

"While within my keep or within the meal lines you will refrain from any violence. You will also refrain from bringing any mining equipment into these areas. Failure to do so will result in..." he pauses again, licking his lips as I pulled the robe down over my pants.

The shirt does fit perfectly, lifting slightly to reveal my stomach. The pants, while covering my legs, leave very little to the imagination as they cling to every curve.

"Disciplinary... action," he said, clearing his throat.

I kneel down, picking up my robe and looking back to the Warden, my spine going stiff as I find his hand adjusting the growth within his pants.

"I will take those dear. Now, you continue down the hall. Tunnel five will be your assignment. Talk to the guard at the pavilion to receive a meal for the day. Do keep in mind that once in the tunnels, it is up to you to ensure your safety. I would very much hate for anything... to damage you."

I stand, feeling the back of his hand push a strand of hair behind my ears. I take a step back pressing against the cold stone wall.

The Warden towers over me, closes his eyes and taking a long deep sniff. Letting it out in a huffed moan, "You may go."

Without another word, I turn, my skin crawling as I feel his lingering eyes the entire way down the hall.

The cavern floor and walls, illuminated by scattered braziers, reminds me of the surface. Each area formed through brute force mining rather than skilled hands. Large tents were positioned a short walk from the bridge.

I approach one of the pavilions with a sign in a variety of languages, none of which I can read. The elven guard inside is snoring, reclined on a wooden chair, his legs propped up on the table.

"Pardon me," I say quietly.

The elf continues to snore. I look around, seeing no other guards. I lean down, knocking on the wooden table. The guard inhales sharply, throwing his legs under the table.

The guard's eyes darken as he looks me over, "Who... what do you want, worker?"

"I just arrived, the Warden said that I should get food here before going to my tunnel."

"You missed meal time, no food today."

"But he..."

"Are you arguing with me, worker?" the guard interrupted, rising to his feet, the chair clattering to the ground behind him.

"No," I gasp, throwing up my hands and taking a step back. "I apologize. I will go."

"Filthy worker, waking me up from my nap," the guard grumbled, standing his chair back up as I walk away. My stomach grumbles as I stare at the markings above dozens of entrances.

One of these has to be five...

Morvina had often pointed to markings that were similar on her maps. Indicating where groups would be positioned. I point, counting out loud as I go, the tunnel on the far left has a single line. I remember Morvina pointing to it, often referring to group one. The next one had two of those lines, the one after that had three. Those were simple enough to count and determine the number. The next one had only one line followed by an upside-down mountain. The one after that was just the upside-down mountain. Morvina had pointed at both of those before, mentioning groups four and five, but they were always together.

Did four have more lines or did five...

"Worker, proceed to your tunnel," a guard from one of the battlements shouted.

I turn to ask which one is five only to see an arrow notched, his bow pulled back. My eyes widen, "Yes sir!" I begin walking towards the tunnels.

Was four lines with an upside-down pointy mountain or just upside-down pointy mountain? I counted the tunnels from left to right again, ending on the upside-down mountain as five. *Please be right.*

The cave entrance quickly narrows as I step inside, startled by the sound of a bell reverberating off the walls. A small rack is formed into the wall itself, holding several sets of large pickaxes, small chisels and helmets with a glinting gem affixed to the top.

I pick up the helmet and run my fingers gently over the gem. "So out of place..." I whisper. Slowly the gem illuminates, getting brighter and brighter the longer I touch it until finally it feels as though I am looking at the sun before the crystal bursts into small flakes.

I hear a rock skitter along the ground, from one of the branching paths before me, holding my breath.

"Oh dear. We haven't had newcomers in quite a while," a crackly voice said from the darkness.

An elderly human woman emerges, dressed in a flowing orange dress that ends just below her knees. A mess of short, curly gray and white hair ends above her shoulders. She shuffles over to me while leaning heavily on a pickaxe, "You don't want to press on the gem dear, you want to tap it instead."

I look to the socket that once held the gem, then back to her.

"Like this," the old woman said, tapping the glinting stone affixed to the top of her pickaxe. The gem responding with a gentle warm light.

"Why are your things different from mine?" I asked.

"Oh, I have been here a long, long time." The old woman paused for a moment, squinting her eyes at me. "Unless you ate it already, I'm guessing the guard did not give you your initial food."

"I..." I begin to say as my stomach interrupts me with a growl. "No, no he didn't."

The old woman lets out a deep sigh with an even deeper frown, "Well come then, we best get a move on before the younger ones come looking for what caused the bell."

"Was that what the sound was?" I ask, grabbing a pick-axe, chisel and a new helmet before gingerly catching up.

"Yes... yes... every time someone enters the tunnel a bell sounds. There are different bells for different things. The Selection, the food call and when someone enters the tunnel."

"Selection?"

"Oh, the Warden didn't tell you? Not surprising. For now, I will just say you don't want to be selected."

"Where are we going?"

"My home."

The web of tunnels feels like a maze, some tunnels branching into a dead end, others twisting back on themselves or leading back to the main tunnel. "I feel like I could get lost down here."

"You get used to it after a few years. Tunnel five is your home now after all."

So it was an upside down mountain! "Do they ever move you to a new tunnel?"

"No."

"What if it caves in?"

"Then you dig your way out."

"But what if you run out of food?" My voice rising with concern.

The old woman turns, gently placing her hand on my shoulder. "Please relax. I know this is a frightening place, but it's okay. Okay?"

I take a slow deep breath, letting my muscles loosen as I exhale, "Okay."

We walk for several more minutes, taking turn after turn. At one point the walls looked so similar I was confident we had gotten turned around.

I was nearly going to say something when the old woman finally said, "Here we are."

I turn the corner and came face to face with a wall. I spin in circles, looking down the various paths for where the old woman had gone. A hand pops through the wall, beckoning me forward. I slowly placed my hand on the wall only to meet no resistance, stepping through it.

Enchantment? My jaw drops, the cavern I step into is filled with a gentle glow. Several gems socketed into the walls and ceiling providing the warm glow in the space. Carved into the stone are several shelves with even more glinting stones. A table with slim benches on either side and two stone beds.

"How long is a long time?"

"Oh, come now. It's rude to ask an old woman her age."

"But this... you made all of this?"

"When I was younger, yes," she said, shuffling over to a shelf and grabbing something that was wrapped in a shirt. She holds it out to me with shaky hands, "Here."

I gently take the shirt, unwrapping it to find a small bread roll. My mouth instantly watering at such a simple offering, "Really?"

"Yes, yes. Eat, your stomach will not allow either of us to sleep otherwise," she said, taking a seat on the bed with a groan.

"Thank you." I carefully take a bit, making sure the crumbs fall into the shirt. While dry and bland, I savor each bit. Picking every last crumb off the shirt. As I swallow the last bits my stomach begins to warm. I look at the woman, still resting on her bed.

"It's okay, don't worry."

The warmth slowly flows through my body, tingling at spots that are sore, simply passing by others. "What?" The pain vanishing, along with the hunger. "The bread was enchanted?"

The old woman smiles, nodding her head, "You know of the arts then?"

"I heard rumors, but I have never seen it. Isn't it forbidden?"

The old woman chuckles, "Oh dear, we have been sentenced to life within these walls. Do you really think that it matters if something is *forbidden*?"

Life within these walls... The thought has me staring down the hall that we had entered this space through. Whatever magic has hidden this cave allows us to see out just fine.

"What's your name?" the old woman asked gently.

"Vera. What's yours?"

"Claire, Claire Woodburn. Listen, tonight, stay here and get some rest. Tomorrow, I will show you where we are allowed to mine."

"Allowed?" I ask, my eyes snapping back to Claire in surprise. "I thought we managed ourselves within the tunnels?"

"In the morning, Vera. I need some rest," she said, rotating her hand on a smooth stone, the lights in the room diming to a soothing glow.

CHAPTER 8

Every muscle in my body aches as Claire leads me through the cold, dark tunnels. The pickaxe feels heavy in my hand. While the, much too large, helmet continues to shift with each step I take.

Claire has been quiet most of the morning. I*s it morning?* Time feels different down here, the gentle glow of the small stones, our only light. I swear I hear footsteps behind us as we cross through several branching paths, but Claire continues shuffling forward with purpose.

"Why can't we dig anywhere we want?"

"It's the rules," Claire says with more of a grit than the night before.

"The Warden's rule?"

Claire stops suddenly and I stumble slightly nearly crashing into her.

"No…" Her squinting eyes stare down the five paths before us.

"What is…"

She holds up a finger to her lips, focusing in on the path to our right. "I have been patient with you. Letting you skulk around behind us. What is it that you want?" My eyes follow hers, unable to see whatever she is looking at down the tunnel.

I hear several rocks shift as a pale-skinned human girl steps into the light. Her short brown hair matted with gray dust. Her bones are visible under tattered clothes. "Miss, I didn't mean… I just…"

"Spit it out girl," Claire snaps, I look at her with a furrowed brow.

"Could I have another stone? Mine… mine broke."

Claire lets out a huff of air, stepping closer to the girl, "I just gave you one yesterday."

"It wasn't my fault. Really, they came out of nowhere. It was everything I could do to just get away." Ice trickles down my spine as I see the genuine fear in her eyes. *She could have been me…*

"Which ones?" Claire's tone has lightened but I can still hear the bite behind the words.

The girl shuffles, looking behind her and then to Claire several times. "I shouldn't..."

Claire lets out a shallow sigh, her shoulders relaxing slightly as she pulls a small clear stone from one of her pockets, holding it out to the girl.

Her eyes widen, a smile erupting across her face. "Thank you!" she shouts, reaching out for the stone.

Claire pulls it just out of her reach, looking deep into the girl's eyes, now filled with concern. "Next time stay near Grug's tunnel."

"I will." Snatching the stone and running back into the darkness.

"Come. Grug only mines a few hours a day."

"Who is Grug? Is he the reason we can only mine in specific places?"

"Grug is a rather large orc that just so happens to care deeply about the women in his tunnel being treated fairly. I think you will like him." She taps her stone a few times, increasing its brightness to reveal a narrow rope bridge ahead. "As for why we have to mine a specific area. Well, it's my rule. If you want to end up like her, feel free to mine wherever you like."

I hear the ropes strain as Claire steps out onto the first board and my stomach sinks. My blood runs cold as I take in the dark void beneath the bridge, "How deep...?"

"Don't think about it, just cross."

"Is... is there no other way around?"

Claire stops, looking over her shoulder at me as she sways with the bridge. "Vera, if you are going to survive down here, you need to trust me. Now cross," she says, continuing across the bridge.

I take a deep breath, holding it as I grip the rope with white-knuckled hands and take the first step. My eyes focus on Claire. On where I need to go. On the solid ground now beneath her feet. Not the fact that the only thing preventing me from falling down an endless pit of darkness is a thin, cracking board.

Claire holds out her wrinkled hand, guiding me across the final step, her gentle smile greeting me, "Good. Grug should be right up ahead."

I hear a deep grunt followed by the sound of metal slamming against stone before the glow of vibrant light filles the tunnel around us. Rounding the corner, I find an enormous gray skinned orc wearing only tattered leather shorts. Every inch of his exposed muscular skin glistening with sweat.

His swing connects with the solid rock, splintering it as a large chuck falls free revealing glittering gems. "This area good," he announces, his words practically vibrating the tunnel itself.

"Thank you, Grug," Claire says, gently patting the large orcs shoulder as we pass by him. I look into his eyes as we pass, seeing the adoration written within them. The corners of his mouth rising around large sharp tusks. *He loves her.* He shakes his head, walking to the end of the tunnel before returning to his digging.

"He seems nice," I say, slowly turning the pickaxe on the ground.

"Thank you, I take that as a compliment." Claire glances toward me, taking in my confusion as she pulls a large blanket made from stitched together bits of orange cloth. "Grug was born down here. His mother did not survive the birth. They rarely do down here. So, I took him in, and raised him as my own and taught him to look after those that can't look after themselves."

My heart aches as I look to Grug, each of his swings releasing large chunks of rock. *A gentle giant, forged underground, unable to walk in the sun.*

"You don't have a chance, girl. Start swinging," Claire snips, now crouched over the large chunk of rock that Grug had broken free when we arrived.

Heat flushes through my cheeks, "I... I wasn't..." I turn, quickly raising the pickaxe over my head in embarrassment. My arms scream as I try to stop it but it's too heavy, pulling into a stumble as I squeeze the handle, slamming into the floor.

I hear Claire chuckle from beside me. Her practiced hands easily breaking free large crystals with a chisel before setting them on the blanket, "What is it that you did on the surface?"

I rub my throbbing head, "I was..."

Witch! The words echo through my mind.

Should I tell her? Can I tell her? Would she discard me? I feel sweat building on my forehead.

Claire's voice is gentler than before, "I was an apothecary before this. My teacher, a horrible old woman, had always told me that it wasn't up to me whether to help someone or not. That being an apothecary meant I could no longer judge people for who they were. I'm not going to judge you, Vera, and you don't have to tell me. I know enough by the collar they put around your neck."

My hand touches the collar, reliving the moment everything changed. "I was Prince Viccar's Mindblade." Tears build in my eyes, knowing that everything I am has been stripped from me. My hands grip the bottom of my shirt as I prepare for her to fall back on her words. *People always lie.*

When I finally summon the courage to meet Claire's gaze, her eyes are warm with understanding. Her lips pressed into a shallow smile. "For now, let's leave the pickaxe to Grug. You can help me with chiseling out the crystals. They weigh a lot less. Plus, it will be good for you to learn what they look like as I teach you what they are for."

After several hours of chiseling, my hands ache. Barely able to hold the chisel in place. A bell chimes twice, vibrating off the walls.

"Wonderful, time to trade in our haul. Grug, sweety, can you please be a dear," Claire says, gesturing to the crystals.

He jogs over, folding the bag's corners together before pulling it up over his shoulders with no effort.

"Thank you, Grug," I say, a smile breaking out across my face.

He glances down at me as he passes, returning the smile as he follows Claire down the tunnel.

It takes us a surprisingly short amount of time to get to our tunnel's entrance, several sets of tools are already resting against the wall. We gently set ours beside them before continuing out of the tunnel. I hear the slapping of feet against stone, turning as my heart drops to my feet. Seven half elf children come sprinting out of the tunnel past me, slamming into Claire as they wrap their thin arms around her.

"You made it," she chuckles, gently brushing their white hair back before reaching into the bag on Grug's shoulder. She hands each of them a large crystal, their tiny fingers barely able to hold it. "Go on now. Remember to get new shoes this time!" she shouts as they sprint down the path.

"Children." The words feel wrong as they leave my lips, watching them run to the pavilion.

"Surely you didn't think Grug was the only one?"

"Who would want to have children down here? Where are their parents?" My skin feels like ice despite the blazing brazier beside us.

Claire's face wrinkles, tilting her head to the side, her mouth opening just as a loud bell rings through the cavern four times. Grug shifts behind Claire, wrapping his one free arm around her protectively.

"Vera, whatever happens while we are up there, remain silent and do as I do. Do you understand? This is very important."

"Yes," I say, following behind them. Even though every bone in my body screams to run.

You can hear the smallest of stones tumble down the hill as we reach the top. The air feels heavy. I look out at the ten people at the top of the hill, all dressed in different conditions of orange cloth. They are forming two lines, women in one, men in the other. They all have their eyes glued to the ground.

Grug begrudgingly releases Claire as she walks to stand among the women. Grug's eyes meet mine, void of emotion as he turns to join the men.

The sound of chains dragging against stone fills the cavern. I rush to stand beside Claire, following her lead with my eyes glued to the floor. The growing sounds of chains are only challenged by the sound of my own heartbeat, ice forming within my veins. I hear bare feet shuffle as tiny feet stop just in view next to mine. It feels as though everyone is holding their breath in unison as the chains suddenly stop, leaving an empty void in their wake.

"No," a low vibrating voice says. "No." The voice getting closer and closer, my heart now threatening to burst from my chest. "No." Black, scaley, taloned, feet click against the ground in front of me. Warm breath that reeks of rot flows over me, causing my stomach to twist and churn. A rough claw brushes down my cheek, coming to rest under my chin. It gently pushes up with its point.

The taloned legs flow into pitch black, tattered robes. The claws extended from similarly scaled hands. It's face shrouded in darkness under a thick, tattered hood.

My eyes widen as deep red and yellow eyes open, digging deep into my soul as I hear it take a long, deep breath. It feels like time has stopped, my chest burning as I feel my throat tighten. *Please... no...*

Shiney crooked teeth of varying sizes form a smile that sends a shiver down my spine. "No." Its voice vibrates my very bones.

I collapse to the floor, gasping for air. The room feels as though it is spinning.

"Stand," Claire whispers, placing a hand on my shoulder. "You must stand."

I pull myself up, leaning far too heavily on Claire for support just as a terrified screech fills the room, "NO! NO PLEASE!" My eyes shoot up, watching the young human girl from earlier being dragged away by the guards, the chained creature following close behind. I can see the entire room, tears flowing down my face as I no longer see the young girl, but instead Iromae's body. Her screams, her desperate pleas for help.

Both lines remain frozen in place, listening to her screams until she is behind the keep's gates.

"Come," Claire says as soon as she hears the doors latch shut. Pulling me towards the pavilion.

Grug is already inside, depositing our crystals into a barrel. My eyes are locked on the keep as I blindly follow Claire's lead. Iromae's screams, her bloody body, burned into my mind. *That could have been me...*

"Come," Claire snaps, tugging hard on my arm as she guides us back to tunnel five.

The events play through my mind over and over. Before I know it, we are back in Claire's cave. She pushes me toward the stone bed. Wordlessly I crawl onto it, cradling my head between my fingers.

"What is going to happen to her?" I ask.

Claire stops sorting the items she must have gotten while we were at the tents. Looking at me with her lips tightly pressed together, "She was selected, I was hoping you wouldn't have to see that so soon."

"What is going to happen to her?" I ask again.

Her lips push up into a deep frown that wrinkles her nose, "The Warden will breed her." She returns to sorting the items, slamming several down with more force than necessary.

"He..." My stomach swirls, my heading spinning right along with it.

"No, no, no, use this," Claire says, frantically shoving a thin stone pitcher into my lap just as I spew bile into it. "There, there, get it all out."

I take heavy breaths. Hoping my stomach is empty as I slowly look back up to her, remembering all the children with white hair. "The children?"

"Most are his," Claire says, grinding some plants in a stone bowl. "The Seer looks into the future, selecting the women that will ensure conception if bred that night. It's how the Warden maintains his, *population*. Not many newcomers are sent down here after all."

I feel my stomach spin again, my brows pinching together, "How do you know that?" I lean heavily over the pitcher, forcing myself to take slower breaths.

"I saved it once. It told me things in return," Claire said, pouring a mixture of plant and water into a cup and walking over to me. "Drink, it will help."

The liquid feels oddly warm as it touches my lips, my head feeling lighter. "Why does the Seer help them?"

A single bell chime echoes through the room, my neck cracking as it snaps toward the entry to the cave. The sudden movement forces me back to the pitcher again.

"Later," Claire says, grabbing a small bag and striding out into the tunnel. "I will be back. You get some sleep."

"How can I sleep?" My words fall on deaf ears as I look down the tunnel to see it empty. I dim the lights, relaxing on the stone slab.

I need to see the sky... the thought echoes through my mind as I dive into my mindscape, searching for the overgrown bridge.

CHAPTER 9

I lay limp on the ground, my entire body aching as I spit blood onto the cave floor. Alice was right, I should have been careful. Then again, I have never been good at fighting and the two men now eating meat at the edge of the cave were intent on it.

My skin tingles as I slowly push off the ground, resting the top half of my back against the wall. The trees block most of it but I can still make out the faint orange and red hues of sunset.

Soon. Soon I will meet my wolf for the first time. *Will I like him? Will he like me?* A laugh builds in my throat, forcing me to cough. *That would give a whole new meaning to fighting with yourself.*

"Alright," one of the men says, bouncing to his feet and walking toward me. "We have time for a few more hits I think." His boot slams down on my stomach.

I roll into a ball, crying out through gritted teeth.

The blows continue until the world feels cold. I can barely hear them laugh as they exit the cave. Leaving me wrapped in the cave's dark embrace.

I force myself to look outside, howls echo all around me. A sliver of moonlight trailing into the mouth of the cave. My vision blurs, the cold replaced by warmth that builds into a burning heat. I roll onto all fours, my skin itching, demanding to be torn off. I crash to the floor, ripping at it. I open my mouth to scream but nothing comes out.

Help!

"We need none," a feral growl resonates with my mind. Everything around me takes on a shade of blue. *"Who hurt us?"*

Images of the two men flash through my mind, their faces, their boots, their laughter, *their smell*.

"Let me out," the voice says, each word laced with rage and power.

I close my eyes, a feeling of safety washing over me. Another howl, this time I don't hear it. I feel it reverberating within my chest. My eyes open and I am sprinting on all fours through the trees. The forest, a blur all around me as my claws dig into the soil. The chill of the night air gifting life to my lungs, every sound flowing into my ears without any thought. There is no pain, only power and strength.

I skid to a stop, my eyes rising to the trees, *"Found you."*

An enormous tan wolf falls from the tree, fangs and claws out. I roll to the side, feeling its fur brush against mine just as my teeth sink into its back leg. The taste of iron coats my tongue as we twist, slamming the wolf into a tree, its bark splintering from the impact.

A twig behind us snaps, I fall to my belly, feeling air rush overhead as another tan wolf flies past, slamming into his friend. I launch forward, snarling as I wrap my fangs around its throat, pinning it against the other wolf, with my claws pressed against its throat as well.

They both shift beneath my hold as I tighten my jaws, feeling my fangs press against the thin skin. A whimper escapes one of the wolves as I feel them both relax. A growl emanates from my throat, they both remain frozen. Slowly I release my hold, standing tall before them. Both wolves stand, keeping their heads low to the ground.

A tingle of warmth flows over me, feeling the pain from where I had bitten the other wolf. *His pain.*

"Good," the growling voice echoes through my mind. Looking side to side, I look to the moon, reveling in its rays. *"Let's find the rest."*

The strength, the power, the complete lack of fear is intoxicating. As if I could survive or do anything. I relax further, letting my wolf take complete control. Trusting him to get us through the night as I feel my mind drift to sleep.

This dream feels so strange, so real. The redwood forest reminds me of home during late summer. The air is warm despite the full moon glow peeking through the branches. My fingers tingle with energy as they brush against the leaves that I pass.

Pushing through the brush, I stumble across a young doe grazing on a berry bush. Its ears perk up, slowly turning its head to look at me. My heart slows, reaching my hand toward it.

Even if this is a dream, you are wondrous to behold so close.

I take a step closer as it continues to watch me, chewing the mixture of leaves and berries in its mouth.

"Hello?" a voice from off in the distance yells. Both the deer and I quickly look towards the sound, then back to each other before the deer sprints in the opposite direction.

"Hello?" the distant voice yells again.

Something deep inside me pulls me towards the voice, carefully maneuvering through the brush.

"Are you there?" the voice yells again. I am much closer now, able to make out the sweetest female voice.

I slow my strides, the most wonderful aroma of warm cinnamon mixed with vanilla fills my soul. The desire to bottle it up and smell it every waking moment, pushing me forward.

I adjust the limbs of a bush, revealing a remarkable half elf woman standing in a small clearing. The moonlight glinting off the strands of red within her blonde hair that flows down to just above her hips. She turns, revealing her sunset orange eyes.

"Where is he?" she mumbles.

"NO!" a deep growl roars in my head.

I reach out toward the girl just before being ripped from my feet, flying backwards at an impossible speed. I slam my eyes shut, my stomach twisting, my head suddenly overwhelmingly fuzzy.

My muscles feel tight, but the movement has stopped as I slowly open my eyes. I'm still in the form of a wolf but the blue hue that colored my world is gone. Richard stands before me, wearing a fiendish smile, his eyes a vibrant yellow.

"Well pup, you made it this far. You are far stronger than your *pathetic* human. I'll give you that," Richard says, looking around me rather than at me.

I look around us, taking in the ten wolves of varying colors. All bowing their heads toward me.

Richards eyes lock with mine, a promise of death in his stair. "Your ascension of the ranks ends here. You are no

Beta. Bow." His words radiate over me, my muscles shiver, my heart racing, the air becomes difficult to breathe.

"Rise!" the wolf within me roars.

I... can't... shadows begin to swirl around me, threatening to swallow me whole. My legs finally buckle, my body thudding to the ground.

Richard's heavy footsteps stop in front of me as he takes a knee. Gently petting my fur as he whispers into my ear. "Too bad the fairies got to that herb witch of yours before me. I would have enjoyed watching you squirm as I crushed her beneath my boot."

A month has passed since that first full moon.

In that time, I have packed on plenty of muscle and gotten fairly decent at fighting, granted I let my wolf lead. Striking when he says to strike, how he says to strike. Oftentimes, just on faith that he wouldn't lead me wrong. He never does.

The full moon pulses energy through my body. It is incredible how powerful I feel when my wolf and I are at our most connected.

Richard and Mia are leading our patrol tonight while I take up the rear. Richard has been extremely on edge, saying that someone has been skirting the edge of our territory.

"Are we almost done?" I ask, knowing that it will irritate him.

"You know perfectly well that we are only halfway, pup," he says.

Mia gives me a knowing grin, "Yeah, it's not like we haven't..."

Richard holds up a fist, causing all of us to stop and crouch low in unison. *Training pays off when it is beaten into you.*

"What do you see?" I ask. The wind is pushing against our back, which makes it impossible to scent whatever he has spotted.

He extends his arm to a small boulder off in the distance, the faintest flickers of orange light glowing off a patch of snow. He instructs us with his hands, sending Mia off to the right as he turns and goes left.

That leaves me as the direct line. I remove my clothes, shoving them into my pack. The white of the snow beating against my skin hiding portions of my new tattoos. It is strange how much has changed in only a month. My blood burns as the transformation starts. It doesn't take long, but with my wolf eyes I can easily spot Richard and Mia in position.

I stalk forward, my black fur a sharp contrast to the white powder all around me. I sink lower, letting it nearly envelope me.

The smell of fire and roasting rabbit licks my snout as I skirt the edge of the boulder. Listening to the humming of the man hiding on the other side.

"Well, hello there," Richard says, walking to the edge of the fire light.

I silently leap atop the boulder, dragging my stomach along its rough surface as I get into position. The man is dressed in fine furs, his red hair curled into wavy locks.

"Who are you?" the man asks, his hand wrapping around the handle of his axe.

Bad move.

"Me and my friend are wondering the same about you," Richard says, holding up his hand to Mia.

"Evening," she says with a nod, her hand resting on the hilt of her dagger.

"I am heading to a town up the road. Just camping here for the night," the man says. The smell of sweat stabbing the air tells me just how concerned he is.

Good, that's smart.

Richard chuckles, dragging his fingers along his jaw, "See, that is the problem. This, here, is our land, and we don't like having strangers just deciding to pass through it."

The man's posture goes rigid as he puffs out his chest, "Really? And what Lord oversees this land of yours?"

"Lord?" Richard lets out a bellowing laugh. "Human lands don't have Lords anymore."

"Check again, King Franklin was crowned last winter. He has been hard at work rebuilding our kingdom to its former glory." The pride in his words overriding his fear from before.

"You hear that, Mia? A new King, how grand. Maybe he will have those little dancing bumpkins like the last one," Richard muses, laughing at his own joke.

"Look, I don't want any trouble. I just..."

"Just need to give us all your possessions, and head back the way you came," Richard said.

The man scoffs, finally pulling his axe free, "Not a chance."

Bad move.

"Have it your way," Richard says, letting out a sharp whistle.

The man turns, expecting Mia to strike at him as I pounce, my paws slamming him hard to the ground as I latch my jaws around his throat. The blood tastes foul, like spoiled meat. I twist, snapping his neck to end it quickly.

Rest now, your fight is over.

Another month has passed. The shadows of death no longer plague me. No, death and I have become good friends. Thirty two, thirty two lives ended by my hands. I can still see their faces just before I ended them. Their confidence quickly dissolving into fear.

"So... what did you do this time?" Mia asks, nudging me with her elbow.

Lately, Richard has made a game of assigning Mia and I to patrol duty. I let him believe it bothers me, but really my wolf is always on edge when he is around. Like that first full moon was never resolved for him.

"I just said hello to Alice," I said with the huff.

Mia chuckles, "You know, for a smart guy, you're really stupid sometimes."

"Maybe I just wanted to go on patrol."

"Well maybe you could do me a favor and try to stay away? Alice is his, you know you need to stay away."

"I'll try. Why does he keep sending you with me anyway?"

Mia looks at me sideways, "What? Don't like my company?" she asks with a smile.

"You're such a tease," I say, gently nudging her with my fist. "How is Ben adjusting?"

"He is doing well, still scared of his own shadow but Lue loves him."

One night, Richard had taken another group to Red River in search of Altha. Instead, they came back with Ben, freshly bitten and nearly dead. Mia was instantly upon him when they arrived. Shifting into her wolf and standing over him protectively. Outside of these patrol details she hasn't left his side since.

"I still can't believe you like him."

"I don't like him... he is my *mate*," she corrects.

"What is the difference?"

"A mate is more than just being in a relationship. You would die for them, kill for them, you would tear your entire world apart for them. They become the reason your feet remain planted to the ground. It's more than a feeling, it's a deep driving need. I *need* Ben like I need air."

I chew on the inside of my lip a little, trying to imagine what that must be like. Sure, I have been with several women since being here, nothing serious though. It's normal after a full moon to feel a bit, *primal*. "How did you know he was your mate?"

She looks to the ground, smoothing the snow with her boot. "There are two signs, first is their smell. Your mate's smell is the most amazing, all-consuming fragrance you can find. I swear both my wolf and I want to roll around in Ben's scent so that we can bring it with us everywhere."

I raise a brow in surprise, "Ben smells like old bread."

"Not to me. To me he smells of old books and candles." She closes her eyes, a large grin forming across her face.

"And the second?"

"You just... know. It's hard to explain, your soul pulls toward them. Once you see them, no one else can come close. As if they were made specifically for you and you for them."

The disbelief written across my face dips into my tone, "Anything else?"

"When you both confess your love, a bond forms between you. For everyone it is a little different but you can feel it connect you. Ben and I can feel what each other feels."

"What's he feeling now?" I ask with a grin.

"A little flustered," her eyes crinkling with her smile. "Right about now I am sure he is trying to get Lue to sleep."

"He is doomed," we both laugh, knowing how Lue is at bedtime. "Why don't you go save him, I can finish up here."

"You sure? Richard might get mad," she says, but her entire body is already moving towards the mansion, towards Ben and Lue.

"Richard doesn't have to know." My wolf purrs, agreeing with every word. "Besides, we haven't seen anyone out here in days."

"See you in the morning," she says, bursting into a sprint.

Want to take the last bit buddy?

"Yes," my wolf purrs.

I quickly strip, tossing my clothes in a small bag and kneel down, the chill of the snow feels nice against my skin as I shift. It always leaves my skin a bit raw, but shifting has gotten quicker each time.

My wolf catches wind of a few rabbits. Choosing to torment them back into their tiny burrows before returning to the patrol path.

It's almost time to head back.

My wolf lets out a huff of steam at my thought, slowing his pace even further. We both love it out here, in the forest, on our own. Well, my wolf doesn't care if others are around, but I enjoy it being just us.

Next time maybe we can convince Mia to let her wolf out for a run.

He perks up at that, turning to pick up my clothes. Just as he lowers his snout, we both catch wind of a familiar scent... *warm cinnamon and vanilla*. With the faintest hint of, *iron*.

Chapter 10

My senses are on high alert as I sneak out of our cave. It isn't a far jog to Grug's tunnel, we agreed to move it closer when I told him that Claire wasn't doing well. He even moved his own living cave closer so that he would be available if needed. My heart aches thinking about how our supply has been reduced to only the handful of black Hematite chunks in my pocket.

I still take the longer path, ensuring I wind around tunnels that loop into each other.

Better safe than sorry.

I hear his pick strike true. A large stone falling to the ground with a *thud* as I round the corner. "Hey big guy," I say, patting him on the shoulder.

"No clear gold stones," Grug says with a frown, presenting the dozens of pre-cracked boulders lining the tunnel.

"Have you been here all night? I thought I told you to go rest." Thinking about how hard Grug has been pushing himself has me concerned. Without him, there would be an even smaller chance to find more Golden Healer Quartz, a clear based crystal with large amounts of deep golden brown mixed into it. It's not rare, but it's also not common. Which in a crystal cave means that it is very rare.

Grug's rough finger brushes away a stray tear from my cheek, "We find more."

I force a smile, nodding my head as I dry my face with my sleeve. I take a piece of Hematite from my pocket, pressing it into his palm. It warms, my fingertips tingling as the crystal's energy fills our every muscle.

"Thank you," Grug said, walking over to the wall and striking it with more force than when I arrived.

I watch him for a moment, seeing how focused he is. Each swing is just as precise as the one before. He would die before giving up on her. I crouch down over one of the boulders, double checking that he didn't miss even the smallest sliver of Golden Healer Quartz. *I can't tell him that I used the last one.*

I stumble into Claire's cave in a haze, using the wall to stay standing as I make my way to the workbench. Pulling out the engraver tool with a sigh. My mouth feels as rough as sandpaper as I place the piece of Golden Healer Quartz we found tonight on the table. It is barely the size of my thumb but it was all we could find.

I reach into my pocket producing two pieces of Hematite, begrudgingly shoving one back into my pocket for later as I squeeze the other. My mouth feels even drier but at least my mind has cleared a little.

I get to work forming the crystal, shaving off extremely tiny chips with unwavering focus.

"You know better than to abuse Hematite," Claire scolds from her bed, her voice dry and rough. "Even the crystals have their limits."

I squeeze my eyes shut tightly, refusing to look toward her. "I'm not abusing it," I said, willing myself to sound unbothered.

"Don't *lie* to me."

A loaf of bread lands on the counter next to me, nearly causing me to snap the crystal at the wrong point. I launch to my feet, spinning around to face her, "What is that about?"

She is perched on her side, looking stronger than I know she is, "Just giving you your rations back."

My rations? Really? I can feel the vein in my neck pulsing as I say through gritted teeth, "You need it far more than I do."

"Please," Claire scoffs, wiping none existent dust from her stone slab bed. "You and I both know that you need to eat something."

"I am *fine* Claire."

She raises an eyebrow, the entire side of her face right along with it. "No, you're bleeding." Her bony fingers pointing to my hands.

Small lines of blood flow down my palms from where my fingernails had dug through the skin. "I…"

"You need to eat dear. *All* magic has a price, the Hematite might grant you renewed strength, but that strength comes at a cost. Come, sit with me."

I reluctantly set down the thin engraver, wrapping my hands in a clean shirt before grabbing the bread and sitting beside Claire, "I'm sorry."

"Oh, enough of that. Eat."

I tear off a small piece of the stale bread, gently placing it in my mouth before washing it down with a splash of water, "I can't lose you too." Tears welling in my eyes.

She sits up, wrapping her shaky arms around me, "Can I tell you something?"

At first, I believed the question was rhetorical, but after a moment of silence I wipe away the tears, looking in her smiling eyes, "What?"

"When I was your age, I had the privilege to know the most wonderful man in the world, Jack. He swept me off my feet and promised me the world. He said we could go anywhere, do anything I wanted. That all I ever had to do was ask. I told him that I just wanted our family." Her entire face wrinkles with her smile, "So he gave me a child. A beautiful baby boy. It was the most amazing six years of my life." She paused, gently dabbing her eyes.

"What happened?"

"Our son always loved to run in the forest, just before dark. Jack told me not to worry. That he could find him no matter where he was, and that he would make sure he was safe. That night, I had just finished making dinner. I went out to the porch and gave a shout just like every night." Claire lowered her eyes, her face turning sour. "I hear his scream every night... Jack was through the door instantly, yelling at me to go inside. To lock the door. So I did. I locked the door and waited by the window." I hand Claire a clean rag to wipe away her tears. "They found Jack, ravaged and bloody. Clinging to a tree. My son, hidden behind him, on the brink of death. For years I told myself it was my fault. That if I had just gone into the village sooner... In my guilt I ran. I abandoned my son, convinced that I was the problem."

"Claire..."

"I wound up here. I thought this was justice for what I had done, that I deserved this. Two months ago, I was standing on that rope bridge. Ready to end it right there. Then I heard a single bell chime." Claire's eyes, slowly locking with mine. "Don't let the guilt over me drive you down that same path."

The world feels heavy as I wrap my entire body around her, gently squeezing, "I'm sorry." Blinking my eyes as my vision blurs.

"Me too dear, me too."

"Vera?" Grug's rough voice says, gently shaking me out of my sleep.

My entire body is stiff as I push myself up. Disorientated as I look around, realizing that I fell asleep in Claire's bed. I reach out, brushing her cheek... *Cold.*

My eyes shoot open, my heart suddenly racing as I rush to the table, grabbing the unfinished Golden Healer Quartz, pressing it against her chest. "Please!" I cry out. "Please!" Tears pour down my face. "Not yet! I need you!" I press the crystal harder, feeling its rough edges dig into my skin.

Grug grips my shoulders, pulling me to his chest.

"No! I can still save her!" I cry out, pushing against his chest.

He effortlessly holds me in place, resting his chin on the top of my head, "Already gone."

My world crumbles around me, as I sob myself back to sleep in his arms.

The next two days feel empty as I float along the motions. *Eat, sleep, mine. Eat, sleep, mine. Eat, sleep, mine.* I don't bother searching for the bridge in my mind anymore. *Even the wolf knew to stay away from me. Everyone that gets close to me dies.*

My eyes travel along the empty shelves, once full of various jars and crystals. I have run through our final conversation over and over, staring at the unfinished quartz in my palm.

I launch to my feet, throwing the crystal against the wall, it clatters against the worktable. My head, spinning with the sudden motion as I stumble to the worktable. I fumble around, looking for the chisel. "Where is it?" I throw my arms across the surface, sending several bowls shattering against the ground. I stand, picking up the small stool to throw next. I freeze mid swing, my eyes locking on a small bit of paper poking out of the bits of shattered stone.

The chair clatters against the floor as I snatch up the small folded paper. I slowly turn it over, spotting my name written along the top.

I unfold the paper, reading the words etched in red, *"Break the chain."*

The walls vibrate with the bells chime, *one... two... three... four...*

I walk toward the chamber, my mind spinning as I approach the bridge. The ropes creak with the boards as it sways from side to side. I reach the center, feeling my entire world shrink to this one place. My heart beat slows as I come to a stop, gazing into the abyss below. *She was here, right here.* I crouch down, my legs dangling off the boards.

I close my eyes, taking a shaky breath as I inch forward. *"Don't let the guilt over me drive you down that same path,"* Claire's voice echoes within my mind.

Tears rain down my cheeks, as I scream out, "Why?" My white-as-snow knuckles grip the rope.

Two arms wrap around me, yanking me to my feet, spinning me around. Grug's dark brown eyes locked with mine. "I here," he says, pointing to his chest and pulling me into a hard hug.

The bells chime again, the vibrations far more intense than before.

"We go now," Grug says, carrying me through the tunnels.

"You're late," one of the guards says. Eyeing us for a moment before pointing to the line.

Grug gives a deep bow as he continues forward.

The Seers vile grin watches as Grug sets me down at the end of the line. It feels as though every eye is upon me, judging me for failing to keep her alive.

"No," the Seer says, walking past the first girl.

They know it's my fault...

"No," the Seers says again.

They died because I was weak...

"No."

My eyes widen, taking in the black taloned feet stepping into view. *I can't breathe.*

"Yes."

My head shoots up, my mouth gaping at the pitch-black talon pointed in my face. The guards grip my arms, yanking me forward. My feet are dragging against the floor. *No. No, not now.*

"No!" My throat tears as I scream, my eyes latching onto Grug. "Help!" His focus glued to the floor, his white-knuckled fists trembling at his side. "No!" I kick out a leg, slamming it into the side of a guard's helmet, sending it tumbling down the path.

"You bitch," the guard grunts, gripping down hard on my wrist and twisting until my arm is locked behind my back. Pain surges through my shoulder, feeling how little effort it would require for him to break it.

The keep's walls surround us, the gate latching closed as we ascend the narrow stairs. They shove me into a room. A single large wooden bed, covered in white linens, takes up the bulk of the space. A rough chain bolted to its frame. The guard I kicked earlier grips my hair, slamming my head into one of the posts. I collapse to the ground, seeing stars as the room spins.

I feel a hand grip my hair again, pulling my face to meet his. I blink several times, making out the jagged bleeding cut up his face.

"When the Warden is done with you, I am going to make you regret giving me this," he said, spitting in my face.

They storm out of the room, slamming the door shut. I grip the bedpost and pull myself up, hearing the rattling of chains as I realize they shackled me to the bed. The room is small, illuminated by three candles that make the room smell of cherries. A shadow shifts in the corner, my eyes shooting towards it. The Seers red and yellow eyes appear, watching my every move.

I spit on the ground, tasting the blood pooling in my mouth, "You were wrong. I won't let him..." I blink several times, my eyes feeling heavy. "I won't..."

"No," the Seer's voice vibrates through me. Its talons clatter against the stone, pressing something cold against my forehead. My frozen blood burns through my veins.

My vision clears, just as the Seer floats across the room, vanishing into the shadows once more.

The door creaks open again, the Warden staring down at me. "Oh, how I have waited for you," he says, the room darkening with each step he takes. "I wanted to enjoy you when you first arrived, but then my men might think that I enjoy doing this." He removes his belt, folding it over itself with a snap.

I keep my eyes locked on his face, training my face to remain neutral. *I won't let you.*

The shadows concealing the Seer flutter as the Warden stands before me, wearing only a thin gray chain wrapped around his neck.

"You should look at me with more respect," he says with a sigh, fisting the chain that ties me to the bed.

I continue to glare into his eyes, letting the rest of the world fall away.

His eyes darken, the chain shifting near my ear. "Fine," he spits, slapping me across the face. I try to roll back but he folds me over the bed.

"I was going to be gentle with you," he says, ripping at my pants. "But I see that you need to be broken." His oily fingers grip my skin.

Every muscle in my body is tightening, burning, demanding. *Now!*

I pull both my legs up, slamming between his legs. He roars through gritted teeth as he falls to the ground. He pulls the chain, slamming me down on top of him. I scramble to push off, trying to get out of reach.

"No, you don't," he grunts, ripping my shirt as he pulls me back on top of him. I thrash, elbowing him in the stomach. His meaty fingers lock around my throat, lifting me into the air. I scratch at his hands, unable to breathe.

Darkness creeps in around my vision. The Warden's face filled with pleasure as he watches me struggle, "That's it, feel how easily I can end you."

A shimmer of light bounces off his neck. I reach out, gripping the chain into a fist, ripping it off of him.

Shock takes his face, "What did..." His words are cut off by a blood curdling scream as black talons rip through his neck. Blood flowing down his body as he falls to his knees, then, finally collapsing entirely on his side. Blood pooling all around him.

My bones shake and I gasp, sucking in all the air in the room at once. Goosebumps form up my arms as the Seer lurches forward, stopping inches from my face. It gently scraps its blood soaked talon along my collar, its voice piercing through my mind, *"A favor is owed."* Before vanishing into a cloud of black smoke. The strength I felt before, evaporating along with it.

The guards from earlier slam through the door. Taking in the sight of their Warden's final labored breath.

"Look at the mess you've made," said the guard with a scared face. "Tell the others the Warden is dead. I'm in charge now."

He walks through the pooling blood, crouching beside me. I pull my legs to my chest, squeezing myself into a ball. His calloused fingers brush along my skin as he shifts my hair aside, "To celebrate, we will have a hunt." His sky blue eyes promising only pain.

CHAPTER 11

I should be overjoyed as the elevator steadily rises, pulling us up through the plumes of smoke and ash. My new set of clothes feel scratchy, parts of my skin still caked in bits of dried blood. The man proclaiming himself the new Warden stands in front of me, along with two guards to either side of me. Each of them is wearing fur lined leather, their hands resting on sheathed swords.

The thinnest of the five twists a bow in his other hand. "Captain..." His word is met with a striking glare, "Apologies. *Warden.* Do you not believe it would be better to do the hunt in one of the tunnels?"

"What would be the fun in that?"

"But she..." His eyes linger on me for a long moment, under his heavy gaze I pull my arms tight against my sides, willing myself smaller. "What if she gets away?"

The new Warden bellows, holding his chest with one hand as he braces himself against the elevator wall. "*What if she gets away?*" he says in a mocking tone. "I tell you what, if we aren't back with her pretty skin by morning. You can be Warden." Poking him in the chest, a deeper laugh rumbling in his chest.

Moonlight fills the cage as we finally clear the smoke. My heart fills with momentary joy at seeing the stars, real stars after so long. The elevator shakes, having reached the stone bridge.

I rub my arms, the frigid air cutting through the thin fabric. My teeth rattle as I am pushed out of the elevator and onto the jagged stone.

I walk along the center of the path, my eyes drifting to the side, the pit below. "*It would be faster,*" my own voice whispers in my ear. "*They are going to kill you anyway.*" I feel my heart pounding in my chest. I force my eyes forward, focusing on each next step. "*You know I'm right.*"

"You're not real," I say, my eyes wide, sweat building in my palms.

"What did you say?" one of the guards says, looking down at me for the first time.

"I can't leave."

"Don't you worry about that. I wouldn't let a little barrier magic prevent our fun," The Warden says, stopping just next to the edge of the bridge and the world beyond. "Hold this." He presses a small black disc, covered in intricate symbols into my palm as a blanket of cold wraps around me, my back tingling with cold heat.

"Good, now watch that first step," he says, shoving me forward with a kick.

Energy crackles all around me, arresting my forward momentum. The mark on my back is burning, tearing with each passing second that I touch the invisible barrier. I scream out in pain, taking a step back. A boot slams against my back, forcing me forward. I hear muffled laughter from behind me, the burning multiplying with each passing moment.

He pushes harder and harder, smashing me against the barrier. The pain overwhelming my senses just as the crackling and burning vanish and I stumble forward, collapsing into the thick snow. Warmth trickling down my back as I look to find bits of red staining the snow around me.

"See, was that so hard?" the Warden asks, leaning over me. I turn my head, glaring into his eyes. "Good, you still have some fire. You're going to need that. It will make the next part so much better." His smile deepens. He reaches down, pulling me to my feet, facing me away from him, his warm breath against my checks. *"Run."*

Darkness is all around me, the tree canopy blocking nearly all the moonlight. My chest and legs burn with each breath as I thunder through the forest, weaving between different sets of trees. For a while their voices had been right on my heels. Now it was quiet, eerily quiet. Deafened by the sound of my own rapid, shallow breaths and my galloping heart. I slam my back behind a tree, searching for any sign of the guards, my *hunters*.

"They're out there. You just can't see them," my own voice whispers in my ear.

I strain my eyes, desperate to see any sign.

"Iromae can't save you this time."

I shake my head, my hands slapping against it, "Shut up..."

"Claire would be so disappointed in you."

"Shut up!" I scream, turning to face the voice, only to see nothing. Heat drains from my face in realization.

An arrow screeches by, grazing my ear as it slams into a tree. I kick off the tree into a full sprint, adrenaline coursing through my veins. *Run. Evade. Hide.* I hear flowing water just ahead, turning toward it.

The steady river is half covered in large chunks of ice. I scan its length searching for a crossing only to see it widen at both ends.

"You won't make it," my own voice whispers.

No choice. I leap onto the closest chunk of ice, nearly falling into the water as it dips down. I gasp as frigid water drenches my shoes. An arrow skitters across the ice next to me. I leap for the next chunk, crashing onto my stomach. My knees slapping into the water. My heart bursting from my chest. Another arrow splinters against the ice, a chunk of it slicing my cheek. I pull hard, crawling back onto the ice and rolling to the center. My chest feels tight, each breath requiring more effort than the last. Another arrow skitters beside me.

"Who taught you to shoot?" I hear a voice yell.

I stand half hunched over, willing my body to run, to jump. An arrow slams into my arm just as I leap. I scream out in pain, landing on solid ground in a roll.

"What do you mean you're out of arrows?" I hear the voice shout again. I roll over, my hand gripping just below the arrow. I look up, taking in the five men staring at me. "Better run half breed!" the Warden shouts, leaping onto the first chunk of ice.

My eyes bulge, every muscle in my body coming to life once more. I grip the bark of a tree, my nails breaking with the effort, my arms scream in pain as I rise. I scan the forest, spotting the mouth of a cave.

"*Just give up,*" my voice whispers.

"No," I grunt, sprinting for the mouth of the cave.

Jagged rocks cut through my shoes as I enter the pitch-black cave. I reach down gripping the Lightstone I had hidden away in my shoe, bringing it to life with a tap. I slowly navigate the damp, moss covered rocks one step at a time. Shouts echo through the mouth of the cave from up above, rocks nearly colliding with me as they fall.

I tap the stone, dimming its light to the lowest setting as I rush deeper into the cave. A branching path approaches, both giving no sign of freedom. I gasp for air, tasting blood in my mouth.

"Half breed. Where are you?" he mocks. His voice is much too close now.

I stumble left. Taking that as my sign, I sprint in that direction full speed, not slowing as I take turn after turn. *I need to run. Need to get away.* I turn the next corner, slamming into something and falling to the ground. My head is spinning as I struggle to stand, looking up at the solid wall in front of me.

"No," I whisper, my eyes widening as I stare back into the dark tunnel.

A low laugh comes from the darkness. The sound of a single sword unsheathing has every one of my hairs standing on end, "End of the line, half breed." The Warden steps into view first, his sword in hand, the men behind him shuffling uneasily, "I promise to make this slow."

My heart stills, waiting for the strike.

A deep growl reverberates along the walls. I should be more afraid but something within me warms to the sound, the familiarity in it.

I watch the Wardens men vanish into the darkness. A mixture of screams and clattering metal replacing the deep growl. The Warden turns towards it. "What is it?" he shouts, holding his sword in shaky hands.

Another scream answers him, the sound of leather and flesh being torn and dragged, bones snapping.

"Who's there?" His voice cracks. He storms over to me, yanking the stone from my hand. He taps it, filling the room with bright light.

An enormous black wolf stands over the four guards' limp bodies. Its glowing sapphire eyes are a stark contrast to the bright red blood dripping from its mouth. It takes a step forward, every muscle taught with power.

Warm pain splashes over me as the Warden's hand grips the bolt, still lodged in my arm, pulling me to my feet, "Even a half breed has their use," he whispers into my ear, shoving me forward. I collapse to the ground before the wolf with a gasp, landing in the growing pool of blood beneath it.

Every bone in my body rattles within me as I look up. The wolf's eyes are locked on the Warden, following his every shift. Its lips rise, revealing even more of its razor-sharp teeth as it begins to growl once more. It slowly steps forward, over me, around me, as if it were intentionally avoiding my exposed flesh.

"No. Eat that," he says, pointing to me. "You stupid beast."

The wolf snaps, leaping through the air. The Wardens scream becoming a gargled mess.

I roll over. All heat draining from my face, my eyes heavy, the world a blur of gray and white. *You were right...*

CHAPTER 12

"*You just know*," Mia's words echo through my mind as I stare down at her body, the taste of blood still lingering on our fangs as I listen to her labored breathing.

My heart is racing, staring at the growing pool of blood beneath her. *Too much blood*.

My wolf kneels down, taking a deep smell of her long blond hair. Alluring before, now? *Intoxicating*.

I can feel our core tighten, our skin heating. The need to mount her, claim her here and now, before anyone else can.

"*Mate.*" Our words colliding together in unison within my mind.

My wolf steps forward, every muscle pulsing with power. With need.

No... she is dying.

My wolf snarls at the thought.

Shift back, I need to stop the bleeding.

Every nerve burns as I kneel as myself once more. Every muscle is fueled by an intense mixture of rage and desire. I slowly crawl over to her, my fingers tingling as they run over her smooth white skin. Her shirt is glued to her back with dried blood, *old blood*. I slowly roll her over, careful of the arrow stuck in her arm. I take note of the multiple cuts and bruises scattered over her far-too-thin body.

"You killed them too quickly," I whisper.

I rip through the dead elves' pockets and backpacks. I pull out several shimmering rocks, tossing them to the side in confusion as I continue searching for bandages, balms, anything that would resemble a healer's kit.

"Who leaves without any medical supplies?" I ask. I can feel my wolf growing restless, the need to kill everything in ten miles pulsing through me.

I rip some of their clothes off, tearing strips of relatively clean cloth from them and begin wrapping her wounds. I break the head off the arrow and pull the stick out, a small amount of blood flows out but I quickly twist the cloth around it with practiced hands.

Good thing wolves get hurt so much. Her back worries me the most, everything else has been minor wounds and should stop bleeding soon, but her back... Removing the shirt is extremely dangerous without having something to wrap it with and a balm to apply.

I rest my wrist on her head, *fever*. A growl rumbles in my chest, my face no longer hiding the rage boiling in my veins.

I stand, rushing towards the exit when my left leg locks up. Forcing me into a weird hop that slams me against a wall.

"Can't leave," my wolf says within my mind.

She needs blood, balms and herbs. If we don't leave now... My eyes linger on her for a long moment, imagining how I might lose my mate only just after finding her.

"Shift," my wolf growls. I can feel his understanding course through me. The need to help save her overcoming his desire to claim her.

I stare at her pale face, "Stay alive," I plead, leaping into the shift and sprinting through the tunnels.

Please...

Frost covers my body as I return to the cave. Her smell permeates the tunnels now. *I would do anything to return to this smell every night.* My wolf ears lower at the thought as we smell the ting of death in the air. I pick up the pace, fearing the worst as I round the corner.

Her chest is slowly rising, the faintest of white plumes escaping her lips.

I shift quickly, embracing the agony of so many shifts in such a short time as I gently set my bag near her. I pull out my mortar and pestle along with several jars of herbs.

"Fever, blood loss and whatever is wrong with her back," I repeat to myself several times. It doesn't do much to relax my panicked heart as I grind the bits of herbs into a slimy paste. I watch each breath leave her lips as I continue to grind, counting the time between each one.

"Good thing you're asleep for this." I tilt her head back, opening her mouth as I pour the foul-smelling liquid in, massaging it down her throat.

That's fever and blood, now for the back. I slowly turn her over, the sound of fabric tearing away causing my face to tighten as the smell of fresh blood fills the room.

Not good, that's bad, I shouldn't have done that. I fumble through my bag, searching for my knife that is nowhere to be seen. Everything around me takes on the familiar blue hue as I watch myself turn away from the bag. I grip her shirt just below her neck and rip it clean down the middle in one smooth motion.

"Thanks," I grunt, feeling my wolf smirk as my vision returns to normal. A mixture of black ichor mixed with blood slowly trickles out of torn skin in an intricate pattern. I dab my finger in the ichor smelling it. *Ink?* Confusion flashes across my face as I wipe my finger clean on her torn shirt. I pull my only water skin from the bag and begin cleaning her back. The blood flows away clean but the ink holds firm.

Tattoo? I reach out, gently dragging a finger along it. The ink comes away, clinging to my finger instead. I look to my hand, watching as the ink slowly begins to crawl up my hand.

"*Old magic!*" my wolf roars within me.

I pull out the small vial of Nitpaw dropping the faintest amount of it on the ink. Bubbles form around it, sizzling as the ink fades away.

I look again at her back, my eyes widening at the amount of ink still clinging to her back. I shake the water skin, unhappy with the amount left.

"I'm going to need your help, and you're not going to like it," I said, holding the vial to my lips and throwing it back.

My wolf whimpers as we shift, feeling the Nitpaw turning in our stomach.

After you, be quick. I can feel the bubbles forming in our throat as my wolf laps up the ink, his rough tongue moving across her back in wide strokes. It doesn't take long, which is good since I begin to hear the sizzling.

Not on her! My wolf turns, spewing the bitter mixture of Nitpaw, bile and neutralized ink all over the floor.

The room begins to feel fuzzy and my wolf stumbles.

The shift back takes far longer than normal, my wolf whimpering in my mind. "Sleep well my friend," I whisper, feeling his ever-consistent presence vanish from my mind. The cave feels darker, goosebumps running along my entire body as I stand naked before my mate.

I begin ripping the remaining clothes off the dead, using any of the still clean portions as bedding beneath my mates back. *My mate.* The thought still feels strange, and yet so right. I haven't even spoken to her, yet at the same time I would do anything, *everything* to ensure she continues to breathe.

I roll her onto her back, draping the remaining clean bits of clothing over her to keep her warm. I brush her hair behind her ear, taking in her gentle face. The faintest freckles scattered under her eyes, framing her perfect button nose, "No one can hurt you now."

I place a dagger beside her, standing as the last bit of my wolf's heat drains from my skin. I feel light headed, bracing against the wall. I grab one of the elven swords, stepping back to the mouth of the cave. My eyes trained on my mate, watching her chest rise, slightly better than before.

"Need to build a fire."

CHAPTER 13

I hear the crackling of the small fire burning beside me, its warmth soaking into the pile of fur and leather surrounding me. I start to rise, each of my muscles instantly giving out as I hiss at the pain radiating from my shoulder and back.

I look around, the cave coming into focus around me. A small patched together bag rests beside the wall, along with several swords and a bow. *I'm alive?*

"*You shouldn't be,*" my own voice echoes through my mind. I look up, seeing myself sitting on a small stone slab. Dressed in my old gray robes.

Everything comes crashing back, the Warden, the Seer, the guards hunting me through the woods, the enormous black wolf bringing the promise of death.

I rub my eyes, regretting the move as lightning shoots across my raw skin. I turn facing myself again. "You're not…"

"Real?" she asks, tilting her head to the side. "What if I am as real as you are?" Her gaze becoming sinister.

A log on the fire pops, drawing my attention just as the sound of heavy footsteps echoes through the cave. I spot a dagger beside me, snatching it and shoving my hand under the blankets just as a tall human steps into the light.

Chunks of snow falling to the ground around him as he kicks his boots against the wall. "You're awake. That's good," he says, his voice low and rough.

I look to where the other me was sitting to find a bare wall. I quickly look back at the man. He is tall, maybe a head or so taller than I am. His shirt barely containing the muscles beneath them.

"Who are you?" I ask, gripping the knife harder as I pull the loose leathers tighter over myself. Becoming very aware that the makeshift blanket is the only barrier between him and my bandaged skin.

His sky-blue eyes linger on me for a moment, a warm smile growing across his face, "My name is Alex. What's yours?"

"Vera," my eyes linger on his bulging biceps that push his shirt to it's limits.

He walks across the room, dropping a small bag next to the fire before adding several logs to it. Sweat glistening off his tanned skin, "Well Vera, how are you feeling?"

"Everything hurts."

"Yeah, you had extensive cuts and bruises when I found you. It's going to be a few more days before you are ready to travel." He pulls out several sheets of thick bark, setting them on the ground near the fire.

"Did you do this?" I ask, glancing at my bandages.

"I did. Are you hungry?"

"No," I lie, my stomach rumbling just as the word leaves my lips.

His brow raises, watching me for a moment. "You should eat. I have been feeding you what I can these last few days but broth only goes so far." He pulls the other bag over and produces a handful of mixed berries and dried meats, placing them onto the bark sheets.

My eyes narrow, looking around the room, "Days?"

"About four now. Some more of the elves came searching, but I took care of it," he states, standing a few feet away from me. "Are you planning on stabbing me with that blade? Or can I sit down beside you?"

I bury my lips under the furs, pushing the dagger onto the ground beside me.

"Great," he says, sitting beside me with the platter of food resting on his lap. He reaches out, holding a berry near my nose.

"*Poison,*" my voice whispers in my ear, my lips tightening at thought.

He pulls the berry back, his warm expression souring. "If I wanted to hurt you, I would have just left you here," he said, eating the berry himself.

My mouth begins to water, my core heating as I watch him swallow. *What is wrong with me?*

"Please eat." Another blue and red berry appears near my lips.

I slowly open my mouth, his warm skin brushing against my lips as I bite down. My eyes close, the sweet juices of the berry flowing through my mouth in explosions of flavor. An involuntary moan vibrating in my throat.

When I open my eyes his face has a silly grin, "What?" I ask, swallowing.

"It's good to see you eat."

I avert my eyes, my cheeks heating under his gaze. I force myself to push past the pain, taking the plate and feeding myself a few more berries before holding up a bit of dried meat, "What's this?"

"Rabbit. The forest is pretty bare this late in winter."

I reluctantly take a bite, moving it around a little before chewing, a salty chicken-like flavor fills my mouth.

"So, the men that were... *are* hunting you. What do they want?" he asks, handing me a waterskin.

"They..." I turn, my eyes drawn to the blood-stained stone.

The voice of the Warden floating through my mind, "*Even a half breed has their use.*" The image of the wolf standing over me, its growl vibrating through me.

"They can't hurt you anymore," Alex reassures me, his soft voice pulling me back to the present.

"What happened to the wolf?" I ask, daring to look in his eyes again. I swear, for a moment they glowed.

"He's resting, what was this collar for by the way?" Holding up a short wide piece of black leather.

My eyes shoot open as I swallow the food in my mouth hard. My hand brushing against my throat, feeling only bare skin. "They said it would kill me if I took it off..."

He tilts his head to the side, his brow pinching together. "I felt some kind of magic but I haven't found one that a bit of Nitpaw can't stop."

I hold my head, suddenly feeling dizzy. "I think... I should get some more sleep."

Alex's rough hand brushes under my neck, helping me lay back down slowly. His faint smell of citrus and spice washing over me.

"I need to get some more wood. I promise you are safe, so long as you stay here."

His smell and the confidence in his words warm my heart as I close my eyes, letting the world fall away.

The darkness of my mindscape appears all around me. Feeling the eddies of minds all around me as I fall through the vast emptiness. I narrow my focus to the here and now. My own heartbeat guides my breath as I slow my descent to a stop. I reinforce my focus, creating the floor to stand upon once more.

It feels nice to be back. My world echoing the thoughts in agreement. I push my thoughts outward, pulling at a connection to Alex. The desire to know him, understand him, discover why he truly is here, why he is helping me.

I find a thin green string, threading it through my fingers as I follow it through the darkness. It seems to go on forever, winding back and forth. As if someone had wandered alone in the dark, leaving this behind in order to find their way home.

I watch the string go taut, the old moss and root covered stone bridge coming into view. The string running parallel to it, vanishing into the empty void. I reach out along the thread, building the connection between my mind and his. Wooden planks of finely polished redwood sprout from the ground, haphazardly falling into place.

The rope bridge within tunnel five was more secure.

I take a shaky step forward, ready for the bridge to collapse at any moment. Just before my foot connects, I hear rocks and boards crack. The sound of roots growing and straining as they crawl over from the moss-covered bridge. Connecting the two as they fill in every gap, strengthening every weakness. Tiny flowers bloom along the roots, morphing it into something innocent and beautiful.

I step fully onto the bridge. Feeling much more confident in its strength as I gingerly hold the smooth railings as I cross.

I am pulled into a dense forest. Enormous red trees shoot into the sky all around me, the canopy blocking out the harshest rays while still allowing a warm glow. It is warm, the sounds of rivers and animals moving all around me. A sense of both chaos and peace hangs in the air as I feel my way through his mindscape.

The sound of crunching snow echoes around me, stopping me in my tracks. The ground is covered in wet moss and dirt, no snow present. *Found him.*

"We need to give her time," Alex's voice vibrates through the trees. "Look right now we just need her to get better. I know what you want to do, believe me I feel it too, but she was going to die..." Thunder sounds from far off, threatening rain. "*Fine.* I will talk to Mia about it. All I know is, I don't want to screw this up."

Who are you talking to?

Alex's voice trails off, deeper into the woods. I follow, hearing the padding of quick, soft steps nearby. I try to spot the source, continuing to run along the path when I collide with a tree.

I groan, my hand holding my head.

"*What do they want?*" Alex's thoughts vibrate through the ground.

"Shouldn't be here," a low voice says from behind me.

I snap around, my eyes wide. The enormous black wolf from the moss-covered bridges mindscape stares down at me with his sapphire eyes. It is relaxed in its posture, its breathing heavy and deep.

I look around, trying to find the source of the voice.

"*Then why are you back here?*" Alex's voice carries through the wind, the trees creaking with his building frustration.

"You distract him," the wolf growls.

My jaw drops, staring at the wolf. "You... talk? All that time and you never spoke to me."

"You couldn't hear," it responds. My head is still aching after the impact.

"Do you have a name?" Wind kicks through the forest, branches falling to the ground around us.

"*Monster?*" Alex's voice echoes through the wind.

The wolf is staring in the direction of the wind, its haunches raised, "Amarak."

I raise my arm, trying to block some of the wind that is now whipping through the trees. "How are you connected to Alex? Are you like me?"

Amarak's eyes turn, assessing me, "Not like you."

I barely hear Alex's voice over the ever-increasing wind, "*I need you! Now!*"

Shadows begin to pool around Amarak, floating up and over him, "Stay safe." The shadows swallow him whole before both he and the shadows vanish entirely.

The hurricane force winds die down almost instantly. I stand up fully, looking around as sunshine beams down all around me. The enormous red trees are replaced by the familiar large brown ones, the ground littered with the blooming flowers and tall grass.

Am I in Amarak's mindscape now?

CHAPTER 14

Perched in the darkness of the tree's canopy, the men below are unaware of my presence. There are no leaves left on the trees but their thick branches have little trouble holding my weight as the wind continues to beat the snow against my face in full force.

The five high elves are all crammed together around a small, poorly made fire that is barely clinging to life. Two of them remain awake, presumably to keep watch while the other three sleep.

My mind is racing at the fact that I have left Vera alone in that cave, vulnerable to attack. My wolf is just as antsy, constantly pushing me to look back in that direction even though we haven't been able to see the cave for miles. I want to, no, *need* to be close to her. To know she is safe, protected, *mine*.

I led these five away, down a false trail that should have led them right to the severed limbs of the ones they are looking for just last night. It wasn't hard for us to make it look like an animal attack, after all. So why are they back? *What do they want?*

"I don't understand why we are still out here," the smaller one complains while rubbing his arms.

"The council is disturbed that we lost not just the Warden, but the captain as well," the largest of the five replies, poking the fire.

"They are dead though. The captain's ring proves that those body parts belong to his search party."

"The council agrees with that," he said, taking a long pull from a metallic flask.

Then why are you back here...

"They don't believe it was an animal though."

"What do they think it was?" he asks, looking into the darkness around him, the sound of his heartbeat ever so slightly increasing.

"Werewolves."

The small one's eyes blanch, a shallow chuckle emanates through his chattering teeth, "You're funny. The were-wolves are all dead, everyone knows that."

"That's not what this says," the man that I now believe to be the leader said, holding up a small blue and green rock, a warm glow emanating from its core.

"What's that?"

"Labradorite. It's been etched to glow whenever one of them is within a few miles of us."

The small one's eyes dart around, practically bulging out of his face now. "Then why are we out here? Those monsters killed the captain and four other guards. What are we supposed to do against that?"

Monster?

"Watch your words boy. If the council tells us to jump in a river, that's what we do. They tell us to go out and kill some legend in the woods, then we do it." He emphasizes the last bit by throwing another log onto the fire, sending embers and ash scattering into the wind.

I roll my shoulders, deciding it would be better to check on Vera and come back later. When they are sleeping.

"Besides, the council believes that they have the half elf witch with them." My entire body freezes in place, slowly turning to face them again.

"The one that the Warden was going to breed?" My blood heats at the thought of anyone touching her.

"The same. Good thing for us that he didn't get to though. It will be nice to have a tight hole for once, before we slit her little throat."

Their guttural laughs fill the air. All I can see is red, the branches beneath me splintering as my fingers dig into them. *I need you. Now!* I leap from the tree, driving the stolen sword down through the leader's shoulder and out his side.

The smaller man screams, struggling to create distance between us.

Claws replace my fingernails as I leave the sword in place, throwing the leader forward. Sparks erupt from their fire as he collapses into it.

Knife. My wolf growls within me, pulling my head back as it glides mere inches from my nose. I dive towards the thrower, running on all fours, as claws tear through my boots. I am on top of my next victim before he can draw his sword, my fangs ripping into his throat.

"Run!" I hear the small one scream as he begins sprinting into the forest. All darkness dissipates as my world takes on the familiar blue hue of my wolf's vision, welcoming our hunt for those that would dare to threaten what is ours.

Finally fully shifted, blood dripping from my lips, a growl builds within my chest. I can still hear the small one's footsteps, his heavy gasping breaths. The other two stand before us, their swords held in shaky hands as they look between their burning leader's corpse and the *monster* before them.

"*My turn,*" my wolf says, letting loose a snarl as he pounces forward, swatting a sword to the side with his paw as he snaps our jaw around the arm, pulling the elf to the ground in a tumble. The other one screams, his boots kicking up snow as he leaves this one to die.

"Don't leave me!" he screams, slamming his fist on our snout.

My wolf tightens our jaw more, the sound of snapping bones and blood-curdling screams fill the air. We release our hold tearing into his throat, erasing his screams from the land.

They're getting away! The small one is heading north, toward the elven city. The other south, toward Vera.

Without a moment's thought we charge south, barreling toward our prey. He is fast, but reckless as he turns looking back at us, slamming headfirst into a partially fallen tree. We are on top of him before he can rise, our claws tearing through his neck.

We leave him choking on his own blood. *One left.* The wind whistles around us as we arrive back at their camp. His tracks have been completely erased by the blizzard. I can no longer hear him, but I rush over to where he had been sitting, locking onto his scent.

I dart along the path, his scent weaving around trees. I dive through the brush, my paws failing to meet ground as I plummet down a cliff face. The soft snow does little to arrest our descent as we tumble, slamming into a tree, with a whimper. I struggle to rise, feeling my ribs dig into my side.

I lift my nose, his scent no longer present. "*No!*" my wolf roars. Trying to run but instead burying our face into the snow as our legs give out.

We need to get back to Vera. I plead, trying to be the voice of reason despite the sinking feeling that he will return with more men.

My wolf snarls, rising to his feet again. *There could be more of them.* That has him looking back south, shifting back to our human form.

The shift leaves my skin raw, but the ribs snap back into place. I remove the tattered bits of clothing still clinging to my skin, the cold snow feeling nice as it melts against me. Every step brings pain as I climb back up the hill, knowing that my wolf blood is working hard to heal unseen internal damage.

I adjust the uncomfortable leathers I took from the dead, annoyed that none of them were even close to my size as I limp into the mouth of the cave.

The frustration melts away as I take in my mate's scent. Watching her shallow, but steady breathes, her heartbeat soothing my wolf with the comfort of knowing she is safe.

I tip toe over, stacking several more logs onto the fire before sitting beside her. I brush the hair from her face, appreciating how beautifully peaceful she is. I gently roll her over, removing the bandages from her back. Relief washes over me to see that the wound is no longer bleeding.

I grab a jar of healing cream from my bag, applying a thin layer to her back. *She shouldn't scar.* I smile, the pride in my chest deflating as I roll her over and take in her clearly visible ribs.

"*Not your fault,*" my wolf reminds me. I sigh, knowing he is right.

Vera shivers, rolling onto her side and pulling the leathers tight around her. *We know so little about her. I want to change that.*

CHAPTER 15

My eyes shoot open as I gasp desperately for air. The flickering light of the fire, warming the cave walls with life. *I'm not in the keep. I'm not in his hands. I'm not trapped.*

I reach back, brushing my fingers through soft warm fur. I slowly turn, finding the enormous black wolf lying beside me.

Amarak. His ear twitches, as if hearing my thoughts. I pull closer, his thick warm fur devouring the chill from my bones. *You were there for me when no one else was.*

I look up. Finding the bark plate filled once more with breads, cheese and berries. I pull it close to me, devouring the cheese and berries with one hand while petting small circles in Amarak's fur with the other. It feels strange to leave the bread on the plate, feeling full for the first time in months. I reluctantly rise to my feet, stretching my sore limbs. The skin on my back feels tender as I move. Everything else feels right again, though. Weak, but I could move if I had too.

I look around the cave, taking in the additional weapons leaning against the wall, several new elven packs beside them.

Where is Alex? Unsure if it needs it, I place another few logs on the fire.

Amarak stirs a little, adjusting his snout towards the fire but remains asleep.

Confident that Amarak would stir if Alex was coming back. I carefully walk to the packs, pulling out an oversized white shirt and underpants and putting them on near the fire.

"*Why is he helping you?*" My voice breaks through the silence, causing me to jump and turn quickly, looking at myself perched on the rock again.

I dive into the darkness of my mind, finding no threads of life aside from Amarak and Alex nearby.

She clicks her tongue several times, "Come now, do you still think I'm not here?"

"You can't be," I whisper. "You're not real."

"You're not real," she mocks. "Why is he helping you? Hmm?" Her hands spread wide.

"He..." I start, realizing I never asked him. *Why is he helping me?*

"Exactly. Look at you. He didn't even bother to put you in clothes when he had them available. He is just keeping you around to use you. Just like the Warden was going to use you."

Goosebumps rise along my arms as my thoughts take me back to that bedroom. His grime covered fingers brushing against my skin. I shake my head hard, glaring at the figure, "No. He isn't like that."

"Isn't he?"

"He isn't." Even I hear the confidence waiver in my voice.

A grim smile crawls across the figure's face, "We shall see."

Amarak whimpers behind me, drawing my attention. When I look back the figure is gone, no trace that it was ever truly there before. Amarak whimpers again, his hind legs kicking lightly.

A smile pulls at the edges of my mouth, my heart warming. *Are you dreaming?* I lay down beside him again. Wrapping myself in his warmth as I cross over the bridge to his mind.

I could use a run in the woods with you.

It's dark in the forest, a cold mist filling the air.

Several howls erupt from all around me. My heart beats in my chest as I push up against a nearby tree.

"Dad!" I hear a small boy scream off in the distance.

My brow furrows, staring into the darkness. *A child? Here?*

"Dad!" the boy screams again.

I stay low, moving through the brush carefully. *Why is a child in his mind?*

The wolves howl again, their howls ahead of me now. My blood runs cold, my eyes wide. *They are going after the boy.* I try to scream out, calling for the child to run toward me but no words come. I try again, feeling the muscles in my throat strain with not even a whisper following.

A terrible blood-curdling scream fills the forest. I charge forward, pushing through bushes, bounding over fallen trees. I hear a deep snarl followed by several whimpers just up ahead. I slam against a tree. Daring to peek around it. Two large tan wolves stalk around another enormous wolf, its black fur shifting with the wind. The moonlight reflecting off its sapphire eyes.

Amarak?

Amarak slams one foot forward, snarling, revealing razor sharp fangs.

The larger of the tan wolves pounces forward. Amarak pivots, slapping it to the side with a paw. The second tan wolf leaping onto his back. He rolls, slamming it into the ground. It's then that I spot the boy. He is tucked into a ball, sobbing within the knot of the tree behind Amarak.

I lunge forward, slamming against an invisible barrier. I slam my fists against it, trying to scream again.

A woman with black curly hair crouches beside a bush just in front of me. Setting down a crossbow as she pulls out a bolt. Dipping it into a small vial filled with a reddish-brown liquid, its stench burning my nose. My eyes shoot between her and the boy. The tan wolves are circling Amarak as she cranks the bolt into place. Aiming it down.

It whistles through the air, slamming into Amarak's side. The tan wolves attack as one, Amarak locks his jaw on one, the other ripping into his side. Amarak lets out a yelp, releasing his hold as they pull away.

I try to scream again, my throat ripping under the strain.

The woman slings the crossbow over her shoulder, running in my direction. I stand in her path, her eyes not even taking notice of me. I widen my stance, the muscles in my arms tightening. *If I can get that crossbow…* but before I can grab her, she collides with the barrier, turning to mist.

A wolf yelps again, pulling my focus back. Amarak's jaw is latched onto one of their legs, twisting hard as he throws it into its friend. They roll to their feet, snarling at each other before charging into the woods. Turning to mist as they dive through the bushes.

Amarak limps to the side. Collapsing the ground with labored breath.

"Dad!" the child screams again, pushing himself deeper into the tree.

The entire forest seems to go silent as I watch Amarak's fur retract, being replaced by tan human skin wrapped over bulging muscles. He slowly rises, the bolt still sticking out of his side as blood pours from cuts all over him. He limps, stark naked, over to the boy, whispering to him before sitting against the tree. Sealing the hole with his back as he furiously watches the tree line.

The night sky moves overhead at impossible speeds, quickly shifting to a mid-day sun. The man sitting against the tree has stopped moving, his glazed over eyes still watching the tree line.

"Jack!" I hear multiple voices shout in the distance.

I fall to my knees, my hand slamming over my mouth.

"For years I told myself it was my fault," Claire's gentle voice says in my mind.

"Alex!" I hear the voices shout.

My heart becomes ice cold, tears flowing down my cheeks. I feel warm fur brush up against me as Amarak rests his head on my shoulder. I wrap my arms around him, gripping his fur.

I'm so sorry.

I pull out of Amarak's mind, the chill of the dark cave biting my skin. I reach out expecting to feel Amarak's soft fur but instead feel warm, muscled skin.

Werewolf.

I snatch my hand back, everything I have been taught screaming at me to get up and run. The stories of them raiding villages in the dead of night, feasting upon their own young. I push to my feet, quietly running to the mouth of the cave. Shivering as the snow-covered ground licks my bare legs.

I look back into the dark cave. A feeling of concern whisps through my mind across Amarak's bridge. Alex's words echoing through it, "*I promise you are safe...*"

"*Everyone lies,*" my own voice whispers into my ear. My teeth grind as I grip my hair, grunting as I slide along the cave wall to the floor.

What am I supposed to do? Where would I even go?

"Can we talk?" Alex asks, his gentle voice caressing my cheek while he leans against the opposite wall wearing only pants, his firm skin reflecting the moonlight.

"Are you a werewolf?" I ask, staring into his eyes as I connect with his bridge.

"Yes, but you already knew that."

Truth. "Why are you helping me?"

His brows pinch together, "Why shouldn't I help you? How do you do that, by the way? Get into my mind?"

Interest... not fear? "I have always been able to do it." I feel his hungry eyes linger on my exposed legs, crossing them tight. "What do you want from me?"

"From you?" He shakes his head, erasing the look of hunger. "I want you to be safe."

Not fully a lie... but... fear? "What don't you want to tell me?"

"I..." Alex sighs, brushing a hand through his short brown hair.

His eyes flash blue. "Mate," Amarak's deep voice growls.

I pull my shoulders together, looking at him sideways.

Alex's eyes stop glowing as he looks at me, a hurricane of concern and fear within his mind. *"See, now that didn't help,"* his voice echoes within his mind.

"Mate?" I ask with squinting eyes. *What does that even mean?*

"I don't fully understand it either," his voice was quick and sharp. "I just know that you're my mate, and I *need* you to be safe."

Truth... My jaw begins to ache as I stare into Alex's desperate eyes, "Can we go back inside? I'm cold."

"Of course," he says, clearing the distance between us in two steps and scooping me into his arms. I rest my cheek into his chest, his heat melting away the icy chill. It feels nice, the way he carefully holds me, squeezing just hard enough. I close my eyes, his citrus and spice scent soothing my pain.

He lowers me onto the leather and fur bedding. My fingers linger against his chest, some part of me wanting to stay nestled in his arms.

"What is it?" he asks.

"Can you... can you show me how to build the fire?" I say with a sigh.

Happiness blossoms across his face as he grabs a handful of logs, completely oblivious to my deception as he begins talking me through their placement. Where to leave gaps, how too much air can be just as bad as too little at times.

When to add logs and when to just adjust them. Soon he has a roaring fire, the cave walls once again bouncing with firelight.

Alex sits beside me, holding a plate of berries out as he chews on one himself. I smile, taking one for myself as I lean against him. *Why do I feel so safe with you?*

"So... My wolf likes you. Which is good, because he is one of those friends you can't really get rid of."

I laugh, gripping my tightening stomach as I watch his eyes smile at his own bad joke.

"Where are you from?" I ask.

"Originally, I am from a small village called Red River, but more recently I have been living among my new pack. They are about a day's walk from here."

An entire pack? "Are they nice?"

Alex scrunches his face, twisting his lips as he ponders my question. "Most of them are, some of them more than others, but I think that could be said for anyone anywhere. How about you, where are you from?"

"Everenthia. It's the..."

"Elven city on the edge of the world," Alex finishes, looking into my eyes with wonder.

I look back to the fire, my cheeks heating, "Yes, well, I only ever knew of the inner district."

"I have heard that you can see beyond the great sea from the top of the palace. Is that true?"

I chuckle, "Not quite, but it is a beautiful view. At night, I would often stand at the top with..." I stare into the fire. Feeling these last few months crashing down around me. The attack on Prince Viccar, Iromae's execution, Claire's death. All because of *me*, because I wasn't strong enough to prevent them from happening.

"Vera?" Alex said, his hand resting on my shoulder.

I feel the genuine concern and care flood across the bridge connecting our minds. The need to know that I am ok, to protect me. Tears well in my eyes, my face raw as he pulls me hard against his chest. I try to hold it all in, my chest shaking as he holds me.

"It's okay," he whispers, stroking the back of my head.

"It's not," my voice cracking as a single sob escapes my lips. I bury my face into his shoulder, feeling the weight of these last few months crushing me.

"You're okay, but that doesn't mean you have to *be* okay," he whispers.

A flood of emotions I hadn't realized I had been holding back all come flooding out. Tears stream down my face as I scream into the safety of his chest. *It should have been me...*

Chapter 16

I clench my fists, willing them to stop shaking as I watch Vera sleep. My wolf is restless, unsure what we did to upset our mate so severely. The overwhelming need to hunt down whatever made her scream herself to sleep in my arms and present it to her when she wakes urges me to the mouth of the cave.

I sit where I found Vera earlier. Feeling the moon's rays shine down on me as I stare back at it. *You made her skin glow with eternal beauty.* My wolf howls within me in agreement.

I look to the forest, knowing that soon enough the guards will return. Vera isn't fully healed but she walked well enough on her own. If I can just get her back to the Pack, then she will be safe.

I shift uneasily, knowing that it's not that simple. She isn't a werewolf. Marcus has made it clear that we are supposed to remain a secret. But she is my mate, that has to count for something. Besides, I already screwed up by not killing that one guard. If they had reservations about werewolves still being alive before they definitely won't now.

The faint smell of Nitpaw tickles my nose. Tracking it with my eyes as I duck down low. *So soon?* My wolf's eyes shift, highlighting the world in blue. I can't see them, but my wolf *feels* them. Their subtle heartbeats quickening as we stare into the tree line.

They know we are here. I creep back into the cave, quickly consolidating the supply packs into one. There isn't much left, but it should last a night or two. I look at the weapons, knowing that I will need speed on my side as I toss a small boot dagger into the bag, leaving the rest.

I take a deep sniff, the Nitpaw still faint, but stronger than before.

"Vera," I whisper, gently shaking her shoulder. "I need you to get up."

"Wha... what's wrong?" she asks, her voice horse.

"More guards are here. We need to leave," I warn, removing my clothes. "Put these on."

Her cheeks turn red as she takes them, turning around to put them on, "Where will we go?"

"My Pack."

"Didn't you say they were a few days away?"

"If we walk. I don't plan on walking." The shift is quick and painless as I land on all fours, shaking the tingling sensation away.

"But I can't..." She turns around, her eyes crinkling with a faint smile. "Oh, you want me to..." Raising her hand toward my back.

My wolf lets out a huff of air, laying down on the ground.

She bites her lip, slinging the bag I had left beside her on her back before climbing onto ours.

My mind feels hazy for a moment, a mixture of thrill and fear that isn't my own fluttering through me as she lightly takes a handful of fur. I look back at her, growling a little as our eyes flick between her hands and her face.

"Tighter?" she asks, with a raised eyebrow. "I don't want to hurt you."

My wolf lets out another huff of air, rising to his feet abruptly.

Vera shifts slightly, pulling herself back up, "Ok, I get it. Hold on."

I feel my every muscle tighten as her breasts press against our back, her nails digging in, tightly gripping our fur.

Hold on Little Elf.

The forest is eerily quiet as we tear through the snow, the faint smell of more guards all around us. I weave through the trees, narrowly avoiding branches that might hurt our mate as I try to push forward.

The cold wind blasts me in the face, a chill running along my spine. *We are upwind...* Shouts sound to my left.

My wolf growling, abruptly changing direction by kicking off a tree. We land hard on the ground, Vera gripping tighter with a grunt.

Careful! I scold.

The tang of magic tickles my nose, forcing a sneeze. The air around us becomes heavy, my thoughts hazy.

"Look out!" Vera shouts, gripping our fur and pulling back hard. An arrow grazes the fur under my jaw before slamming into the tree beside us.

My wolf snarls, revealing our fangs while looking for the attacker.

Elves step out from the trees surrounding us, their bows creaking with knocked arrows. I feel Vera shiver, her chin digging into our neck.

An elf dressed in fine, polished armor steps into view. His hand resting on the gem encrusted hilt of his sword, "I would recommend against fighting or running further." His voice is sharp and clear, filled with confidence.

My eyes track each guard, their muscles shaking as they hold their aim. The pair to the right, slightly farther apart than the rest.

"I'm sure you are thinking that there is a way out of this," he says, stepping closer to us. "I assure you that you're mistaken. By now you should be feeling the effects."

My vision blurs, my strength beginning to wane. Forcing me to widen my stance. *They put Nitpaw in the air?*

"We have more men in the surrounding area. Even if you did get through us, you wouldn't get far."

"*He's lying,*" Vera's voice echoes in my mind. Confusion courses through me but I can feel the certainty behind her words.

"We just want the girl. You give her up and you can crawl back into whatever hole you crawled out of."

My wolf growls back. Several of the guard's twitch, sending arrows flying into the sky.

Now!

We spring forward, Vera scrambling to get a better grip as we charge through the armored guard. He struggles to pull his sword, cursing as he dives into the snow.

Arrows whistle through the air as we leap over him, pushing for the gap to the right. The smell of magic is burning my nostrils. Another round of arrows flies through the air. I feel a sharp pain in my side, pushing it to the side as I focus on the closing gap ahead.

"Stop them!" the armored guard yells.

The two guards are there now, frantically nocking another arrow as I barrel forward.

"No!" Vera screams. Blue crackling energy shoots forward, colliding with the guards in an explosion of blood and snow. I feel Vera burrow into my fur, her entire body shaking. I charge through the mist of blood and snow, the taste of death coating my tongue as we push down the hill.

The shouts of the guards are distant as we reach the bottom. The darkness of the forest masking our presence as I come to a slow, my vision returning to normal as my wolf's connection wavers.

Hold on buddy.

I force my muscles to continue at a trot for a few more miles. My lungs are on fire when I find a decent cave entrance blocked by several boulders.

Vera slides off, leaning heavily against me as I begin pushing rocks to the side, widening the entrance.

"I can't..." Her hand rubbing deep into my fir, pain surging through me, "You're hurt..."

My face and limbs feel cold as I look up. My vision is blurring as I see her hands soaked in blood. *My blood.*

The smell of magic fills the air as I lick my nose. My head nestled in Vera's lap as her tired eyes look down at me.

"Hey," Vera coos. "Next time you are going to collapse, can you do it in the cave?" Her smile widening as she pets my fur.

I struggle to rise, her hands pressing me back down.

"No, stay still. I did what I could with what we had but you need to wait a little longer for the crystal to finish its work."

My eyes flick down, spotting her hand resting on my side. A warm yellow light glowing through the gaps in her fingers.

"I'm surprised that you kept them since you clearly didn't know what they were for."

Happy accident. I think, my heart warming as I lay my head back into her soft lap.

I can feel the residual effects from the Nitpaw still in my system, my wolf still in a deep slumber within me. *I would do it all again if just for this.*

"More like his dumb luck saved him again," Mia said, dumping a bundle of wood against the wall. Her vibrant yellow eyes glaring at me as she sits next to the fire.

"Your friend found us shortly after you collapsed. I'm glad too, because I could barely move you and the hunters were closing in," Vera said, watching Mia with a tinge of fear.

A growl begins to form in my chest as I look back to Mia.

"Hey, none of that. It's not my fault the tiny elf is scared."

"I'm not scared," Vera defends, her brow tightening as her hand digs into my fur more.

Mia chuckles, tossing another log on the fire. "You put on a good show, but every time I walk into the cave you start sweating and your heart rate increases." She looks at me for a long moment, letting out a deep sigh before looking back to Vera. "It would help me a lot if you would relax though. That way my wolf stops thinking something snuck in here."

I let out a shallow whimper at the momentary lapse in her petting me as Vera straightens her already straightened shirt.

Mia raises an eyebrow at me. Her eyes return to their normal blue as she exits the cave again, visibly shivering.

I can't help my widening smile as Vera continues to pet me while we wait for the crystal to finish its work. I feel better than I have in weeks, but I don't want this to end. I would stay like this forever if she would let me.

"I need to tell you something..." Veras says, snapping me out of my bliss. "But I don't want to hurt you." I lift my head, my nose inches from hers. "I can enter people's minds. While there I can feel, hear and sometimes even see their thoughts. If I am careful... I can do it without them knowing." She leans to the side a little, looking down the tunnel and chewing on her lip before continuing. "I used to use that power to protect Prince Viccar of Everenthia. One day I was attacked by someone with similar gifts, they forced me to attack him... That's why they are hunting me, and I don't think they are ever going to stop."

Mia's footsteps fill the cave as she walks back in, dumping another load of wood in the stack with a heavy sigh. "Well, I think we have plenty of wood for tonight. You need to get some sleep girly, and you." Mia jabs a finger toward me. "Follow, we need to talk."

"He isn't..." Vera begins to protest.

"He is fine, you get some sleep. We will be just outside," Mia says, not waiting for a response before going back outside.

I look up at Vera, her pleading eyes making me not want to leave. I nuzzle against her neck, letting her squeeze me tight before following Mia into the cold.

I find her leaning against the rocks, staring into the tree line. "Here, get dressed," she says, tossing a leather bag to the ground in front of me.

It feels strange, shifting back after having been in my wolf form for so long. Like being in a ball all day and suddenly stretching out. The dark, tattered clothes fit well enough but itch a little against my raw skin. "How mad is he?" I ask.

"He thought you finally took off for that damn village of yours, took half the pack there to hunt you down."

"Did they hurt anyone?"

"You weren't there, so no. Who is she?"

"She's my mate."

Mia holds her breath, looking at me for a long moment. A sly grin stretching across her face, "You sure?"

"Yeah, yeah, I know," I chuckle, laughing at the irony.

"Has the bond snapped into place yet?"

"No... To be honest, I don't know what I am doing here Mia."

"No one does, just give it time. I will admit though, I haven't seen someone mate with a non-wolf before. I've definitely never heard of a cross species mate."

"She drives me crazy Mia. Every second I am away, my skin burns, I feel like I would do anything just to hold her in my arms for another second."

"How does your wolf feel?"

"Like he would kill anyone that dared to look at her the wrong way."

"Mine is the same way with Ben. It's their primal need to stake claim to what is ours. Now that I know she is your mate it makes a lot more sense why she was acting so weird."

"Weird?" I question with a subtle growl.

Mia gives me a sideways glance, rolling her eyes. *Maybe not so subtle.* "You are clueless. Ever since I found you two and pulled you into the cave, she hasn't taken her hands off of you."

I laugh, nudging her in the shoulder.

"I'm serious Alex. She sees me as a threat, whether she wants to admit it or not."

I stare into the tree line, my chest tightening, "I worry she won't accept the bond."

"Give it time," Mia offers, giving me a sympathetic look. "But for now, we need to do some damage control with Richard. Tell me what we are up against."

Chapter 17

The tips of my fingers still ache from the other night. The fact that this time I conjured that blue energy on my own. It wasn't as focused, but its raw power, the explosion that it caused? A shiver runs through me at the idea that I have that much power within me and no understanding of how to control it.

"What is it?" Alex asks from beside me. The glow of the fire highlighting his honey colored hair.

"Nothing," I say, taking a bit of cheese to hold off talking further.

Alex's brow tightens, a subtle frown forming across his face. "You should know that while I can't read your mind, lying to a werewolf is pointless. Or you at least need to weave some truth into it."

I give him a glare, swallowing hard, "I'm not lying."

He chuckles to himself, "I can hear your heart skip a beat every time you lie. Smell the sweat building on your palms when I ask a question you don't want to answer. If you don't want to tell me, that's fine, just don't lie."

I wipe my hands down my shirt, my eyes lingering on my lap for a moment, "I'm just thinking about the other night."

The silence builds in the cave as I feel my legs start to go to sleep. I stretch them out, hissing as the pressure builds, the blood pushing its way through the limb. I can feel Alex's eyes linger on my every move.

"I don't want you to get hurt for me," I confess, the words feeling weird when I say them aloud. Alex stops chewing, his eyes void of emotion as if waiting for me to continue, so I do. "Too many people have died for me, *because* of me already."

Alex's beautiful blue eyes are locked with mine, whispers of care floating across our mental bridge, "You said you can connect our minds. Can you show me?"

I pull my head back a little, "Show you what?"

"These people you say died because of you. Show me, because I felt the way you trembled when you killed those men last night. You felt bad for them, even though they were trying to kill us, kill you." His face is firm, his eyes pinning me in place. "Prove to me that you aren't worth it."

I feel a chill run up my arm, the hair on my neck rising as I lower my head. *What if I show him and he does leave?*

The edge of his finger presses against my chin, gently pulling my eyes back to his. "Please, show me."

I dive into my mind, standing beside the bridge connecting our three minds. My hand gently caresses the stone, its beautifully coarse surface giving me strength. I step to the edge, reaching out and taking hold of his mind. With a tug I pull him across the bridge.

He looks around, his surprise radiating through my mind like a river as he takes in the darkness of my internal world.

"It's so... quiet," his words echoing around us.

"Being within a mindscape is more thought than action," I say, willing my words to stay quiet.

He turns around, looking at the bridges, "These go to me?"

"You and Amarak." I reply, pointing to each one in turn.

"Amarak?"

I give him a curious look, "Your... wolf?"

A large grin forms over his face, looking at the bridge, "I didn't even know he had a name." He lets out a sigh, turning back to me, "Shall we?"

"If you want to leave, all you have to do is cross back over that bridge."

"I won't."

I build a barrier around Alex, a white circle forming around him, "Stay within the circle, and the memories can't hurt you."

"Will they hurt you?" Concern rippling out around him.

"No," I lie, knowing that memories can cut just as deep, deeper even, than moments themselves.

I let myself relax, floating into the air as I reach over the wall where I keep my painful memories hidden. Pulling one out at a time.

The attack in the military ward hits first. The guards lining the path, terror radiating from them as we walk by. My panic, as the obsidian castle walls trap me within my mind. My attacker forcing me to watch as he uses my own body to attack the prince. The memory fades away, replaced by the smooth sandstone prison cell, Iromae's final words to me before being sent to the Hall of Truth.

I feel the memories moving faster, bubbling over the wall as I try to hold them back. The trial is over quickly, the Queen's demand for justice despite my innocence. We fly through the air, slowing only to see Iromae's lifeless body hanging before we are plunged into the mines. Claire greeting me at the entrance of tunnel five.

I choke on a sob, desperately trying to hold back the memories of Claire. I am sitting beside her on her bed as she retells the death of her husband.

"No," I whisper, looking at Alex as he watches her tell me about her regrets on abandoning her son, her thoughts on killing herself.

He crosses his arms over his chest, his face painfully neutral.

My screams cascade around us as we watch Grug pull me in, holding me as I cry over Claire's death.

The memory of the Seer spills over the wall next. It's terrible smile as it selects me. The Warden's grime covered hands ripping at my clothes. Unable to watch, I turn to Alex. His eyes glowing, his muscles bulging as blood drips down his arms from where his nails have torn into flesh. The Seer's screech tears through my mind, the Warden collapsing into a pool of his own blood. The captain bursting through the door as he calls for the hunt.

The final memory crashes over the wall, my fear, panic, pain all flooding the space as I watch myself cower in the cave. The captain promising to kill me just before Amarak arrived.

I push my walls back up, reinforcing them as I float back down to Alex. He steps out of the circle, pulling me against his warm chest before my feet even touch the ground.

"None of it is your fault," he proclaims.

"It is," I sob.

He pulls away, just enough to look into my eyes, "You said it's all about thought here?"

I nod my head, tears streaming down my cheeks.

Alex kneels down, pressing his hands against the solid ground. A single luscious red rose grows up between his fingers. "The rose is a delicate flower. Its vine, covered in thorns that can cut with the slightest effort." He brushes his thumb against the vine, a droplet of blood coating the thorn. "Yet so many view it as the flower of love. If left in the dark, abused by those around it the rose will wilt, turn yellow and die." The rose following suit with his words. Alex raises his eyes to mine, his eyes squinting slightly. "Yet it is still a rose. If cherished, and taken care of properly it will come back, stronger and more beautiful than before." Alex slowly stands, the flower growing to my height, the main stock strong and covered dozens of buds that blossom into beautiful crimson.

He steps close to me, the edge of his finger pushing my gaze up to meet his once more. "You are my rose Little Elf, but you are so much more."

I blink, the entire world around us transforming into a vibrant forest filled with more color and life than either of theirs.

"When I look at you. I see the golden rays of the sun, gently caressing the entire world. I see the generations old trees, strong and resilient. I see the rivers that bring life to everything around us. It was as if you were born of the sun, and I was forever the moon, chasing you. Forever drawn toward you, but unable to catch you. Now that I have you, I would do anything, become anything in order to keep you."

He leans in, my body frozen in place, a tornado of uncertainty and need butterflying within my stomach as our lips touch. His warmth courses through every part of me. My lips tingling as he pulls merely a breath away, "I love you."

My heart pounds in my chest as I stare into his eyes, "I..."

"Am I interrupting something?" Mia's voice burst through my mind. Our link crashes down, as we are pulled back to the cave. The silence of the cave is deafening as I look at Alex. I swallow hard, following his glaring stare back to Mia.

He said he loves me. That he would do anything for me.

"Yes *actually*. You are," Alex grits out, not trying to hide his irritation at all.

How can he mean that? After what I just showed him...

A devious smirk grows across Mia's face, "I led the elves on a false trail, but it won't take long for them to figure that out. We need to go while we can. If we leave now, we should make it to the mansion by nightfall."

"Vera?" Alex says.

"Huh?" I gasp, looking up in surprise.

"Are you ok?"

No. You just said you loved me. When I showed you why you should run away, *far* away. "I'll be okay, feeling a little dizzy."

"Either Alex or I can help you walk but we need to go," Mia says, kicking out the fire.

"Mia, can I walk with you?" I ask, watching Alex's entire body go stiff.

Mia must see it too since her mouth is hanging slightly open, her eyes cautiously watching for Alex's reaction. "Sure," she murmurs, finally breaking the awkward tension. "Alex, you take up the patrol then."

Alex doesn't say anything, walking deeper into the cave with an empty sack. A few seconds later he walks out as Amarak, the bag now presumably filled with clothes. His eyes look sad as he prances by, dropping the sack with the rest before sprinting out of the cave.

"Well," Mia offers with a sigh, scooping up the majority of the bags. "Let's get moving."

Mia guides us along a path where the snow is heavily packed down. The sun beating down on us from high above. Every once in a while, we can hear the thundering of paws against the snow as Amarak continuously runs wide circles around our path.

"What is he doing?" I ask, needing the silence to be over.

"Our wolf nose and eyes are way stronger than our human ones. He is ensuring that no one sneaks up on us and that we aren't walking into any traps."

"Ah."

"So why me? Why not him?" Mia asks, before taking a pull from her waterskin.

"No reason," I lie.

Mia raises an eyebrow, looking me up and down, "What did he do?"

Right... you can't lie to a werewolf. "He said something crazy," I say.

She chuckles to herself, holding the waterskin out to me, "He does that a lot, I'm afraid."

"Have you known him long?"

"Long enough. He is a good guy. A little stupid, but a good guy."

I take a drink myself, handing it back. "Are you sure it is safe for you to bring me to your Pack? They will just follow us there."

"Safe? Probably not. Honestly, I am not worried about those elves. They seem poorly organized and sloppy. Besides, your Alex's mate. I couldn't get him to leave you behind if I wanted to. Which I don't, by the way."

"Even if it puts him, all of you, in danger?"

Mia looks back at me with a puzzled expression, "Especially then. Look, you're his everything now. I know that might seem a little intense when you just met him, but trust me. There are far worse people you could be mated to."

I reach out to connect with her mind, feeling a barrier of resistance. Powerful resistance, as if some other force was preventing me from forming the connection.

"What does being mated even mean?" Irritation building in my voice, resigning to the fact that I won't get past whatever is protecting her mind.

"Now that is a good question. Let me tell you what it means for me and my mate, Ben." Her voice rising to match the smile now plastered across her face.

Chapter 18

It feels like crossing into another world as we transition into the thick redwood forests of the human land. The beautiful red and orange of sunset dancing through the air.

My heart sinks into my stomach, knowing that I have not only left Everenthia, but the entire elven kingdom. To think just a few months ago I was dreaming, losing sleep even, over the idea of venturing beyond those great walls.

"You need a break?" Mia asks, leaning against a tree.

How is she not tired? My calves are burning, snow clinging to every inch of my pants. My lungs feel like they are ready to explode. Meanwhile, she appears to be just as ready to walk as we did when we started.

"Yes. A break. Would be good." I get out between breaths. I swallow hard, feeling my throat tighten further as I reach for my waterskin.

Despite her inability to get tired, I have enjoyed walking with Mia. Learning about how her mating bond with Ben formed. About their daughter Lue. It really made me question what I had learned about werewolves. It's hard to picture monsters raising children after all.

"No problem, we are nearly there, I wanted to switch out with Alex anyway."

"Why?" I ask, feeling a little nervous. I haven't spoken to Alex since the cave. That doesn't mean I haven't been freaking out about what to say. Or rather, what *he* might say. I tried to feel across our bridge but that same force that stopped me from connecting with Mia is there. It isn't as strong though. I can't hear any thoughts, but I can still feel the faintest bit of his emotions leak through. Mostly fear, shame and *regret*.

"We are maybe ten minutes from the mansion. It will be way better for you if Alex is walking with you when we get there."

I give her a curious look, "Should I be worried?"

"Not if you're with Alex," she states, dropping her gear next to the tree and stripping right in front of me. I avert my eyes, trying to give her some privacy.

Mia lets out a deep laugh, "Oh sweety. Is that why he went into the dark to shift? You are going to need to get over that."

"I'm just giving you privacy."

"Doesn't exist when you live with wolves. We hear and smell everything that happens, no point in being bashful when we know who slept with who and when."

Mia lets out a deep breath just before the sound of several bones snapping has me cringing. Within a few seconds it's over though, the sound replaced by ruffling of fur.

Her wolf isn't as large as Amarak, but it is beautiful. A lush brown coat with black markings around her ears and shimmering yellow eyes. She watches me for a moment with those eyes, her wolf panting as her tongue hangs out the side.

"You're beautiful," I remark.

Mia barks, snatching up a small leather bag with her teeth and dashing into the forest with amazing speed.

I dig into some of the dried bits of meat. It doesn't take long for Alex to return in her place, bringing with him a mixed aura of uncertainty and safety.

"Hey. Can I have some?" Alex asks, picking at one of his fingers.

"Sure," I reach into the bag, taking a handful and dropping it into his palms. His eyes still look a little sad, but I feel the faintest wave of relief push across our bridge.

"How was your talk with Mia?"

"Don't you already know?" I ask, a slight sting to my words. He hides it well but I can feel the pain I caused trickle across the bridge, causing guilt to take root in my stomach.

"No. I kept a wider patrol to give you some privacy," he says, throwing a handful of meat into his mouth.

"She's nice. Why did she say I need to stay next to you when we are there?"

Alex chews a little quicker, using water to wash it down as he swallows, "You don't need to *stay* next to me. But it will be safer if you are next to me when we get there."

"Why?" I ask again, annoyed that he didn't just answer the question.

"Because you are beautiful Vera, and most of the guys at the mansion haven't even met an elf before. You will be... *exciting* for a lot of them."

I feel my cheeks heat a little, thankfully they are already red from the cold so he shouldn't notice, "And by walking in with you, that tells them that I am *yours*."

"Yes," he confirms. His voice is tight, his teeth grinding. "I will also tell them that you are off limits."

My blood begins to boil, the words erupting before I can think, "What if I don't want to be yours?"

His eyebrows pull up together, the rest of his face falling. "I..." He turns away from me, bracing himself against a tree. "Is that how you feel?"

I feel every ounce of fire extinguish within me. His now cold, emotionless words cut through me. *Yes Vera, hurt the one guy not trying to hurt you.* I step closer to him, placing my hand on his arm. "No. You are trying to help. I just... I don't know what I want right now."

He looks at my hand, a faint glow hidden beneath his eyes. "I won't force you to do anything you don't want to. Just know that Richard and Marcus do not have to listen to me. They are my Beta and Alpha, and their word is law."

"But everyone else listens to you?"

"Yes, my wolf... *Amarak*, established himself as third in the Pack. Usually, our wolves don't hold absolute control over pack position. Mine is an exception."

A smile forms across my face, thinking back to my first meetings with Amarak. How the wolf I soothed so quickly the second time around is stronger than the rest. "Well, we will have to play it by ear with them."

The hair on the back of my neck raises, as if my body is aware of something watching us. Alex's shoulders pull back, his entire frame feeling larger by the subtle movement as we pass through a set of trees. I hear the ruffling of several bushes around us, a rugged looking man in tattered clothes appearing before us.

"Alex," the man greets, lowering his gaze to the floor before locking eyes with me.

Alex steps in front of me, "Ben. Mia should be coming up shortly. Is Richard around?"

Even without forming connections between them I can feel the air get heavier as I peek out around Alex. Ben pulls in his shoulders, bowing his head ever so slightly. He somehow feels smaller than Alex despite being a few inches taller than him.

"No, Marcus took him out on a hunt and they haven't returned yet. We believe they should return tonight." His eyes shift back to me.

Alex steps to the side, resting his hand on my shoulder, "This is Vera. Vera, this is Ben, Mia's mate."

I step forward, shrugging off Alex's hold, "It's nice to meet you. Mia has said good things," I say with a warm smile, holding out my hand.

Sweat begins to build on Ben's forehead, his eyes darting between Alex and my outstretched hand. "I'm lucky to have her," he says through baited breath, gently gripping my hand before taking several steps back. I make a note of how heavily calloused his hands are, despite his young age.

"Have whoever is supposed to replace you in a few hours take over now. I know Mia would love some time with you after a few nights apart."

"I will. Thank you," Ben says, turning quickly and jogging down the path.

"What was that about?" I ask once Ben is out of sight.

"What?" Alex asks, looking puzzled

"He looked at you as if you were going to kill him."

Alex lets out a sigh, rubbing the back of his neck. "My fault, I am finding it harder to hold back with you here. Dominant wolf emotions bleed out when at extremes, Ben was having a hard time because I was not doing a good enough job at holding back my wolf's... *our* anger."

"You barely even talked... What did he do to upset you?"

"It's not what he said, it's how he made you feel," Alex says, adjusting the bags on his back.

"How exactly did I feel?" I ask, irritation building in my voice as I shoot daggers at him with my eyes. "Because I don't remember telling you that he made me feel any certain way."

Alex raises his hands, taking several steps back. "I heard your heartbeat quiver. I saw your entire body tense. He made you..."

"Stop," I interrupt, shoving a finger into his chest. "Don't try to analyze me with your werewolf ears. I felt like someone was watching me, and yeah, I got spooked. That didn't mean I needed you to come save me. If I need you to scare away a big bad wolf with your big bad wolf, I will let you know. Ok?"

A wide grin forms across Alex's face as he lowers his hands, "You got it. Can we get to the mansion now? I'm hungry."

My mouth is watering as I tear into the boar leg. The flavor overpowering my need for proper table manners as the juices run down my face and drip into my lap.

I can feel the daggers shooting at me from Alice, a girl that Alex indicated was the Omega of the group. Supposedly she makes people feel, *happy?* I don't see it.

Alex laughs beside me. I follow his gaze to find a man drenched from head to toe. Another holding a barrel upside down over his head.

"Get over here!" the drenched one yells, chasing the other around the yard as the crowd joins Alex in a roar of laughter.

Watching this seemingly normal group of people talk, laugh and play has me questioning the stories. They couldn't possibly be talking about these werewolves.

The memory of Amarak snarling at the Warden as he slowly padded through a pool of blood flashes before me. Reminding me that they are not simply human. Perhaps the stories aren't all wrong, but they are definitely missing key details. Details that if removed, cause them to be seen as nothing more than beasts.

I can't help but smile and laugh myself as I watch Lue, Mia's child, laugh and clap along with the group. Her face and hands were somehow covered in far more food than she had when she sat down.

I take another bite of the boar legs, my eyes flicking back to Alex to find him staring at me. His smile sent waves of heat fluttering through me. "What?" I ask with a mouth full of food.

His eyes linger on my neck as he takes a deep breath, "Your laughter is the most beautiful sound I have ever heard."

I feel my cheeks heat, and know that this time I can't blame the cold. He reaches out his hand, gently brushing a few strands of hair behind my ears.

Alex's face tightens as he looks to the side of the mansion. "What?" I ask, noticing that everyone else is also looking that way. The two men that had been chasing each other calmly walk back to their seat, the happiness draining from their faces.

Two large, well-built men appear from around the corner. The first is wearing a leather coat, with no undershirt and a small portion of a tattoo showing on his chest. The other is slightly shorter than the first, his brown hair shaved close to his head.

Alex stands, gently guiding me to do the same as they walk over to us. I feel goosebumps ripple across my body as the second one's eyes crawl over me.

"Alex, I see you brought someone home with you. Care to introduce us?" The tall one asks.

"Marcus, this is Vera. Vera, this is Marcus, my Alpha."

"Oh, come now, we are more than that by now, right?" Marcus says, slapping Alex on the shoulder. "I took him in when he had nowhere else to go. A stray pup lost in the woods."

"How kind of you," I say, feeling Alex's resentment for the man trickle across the bridge. The man beside Markus, clears his throat, watching Alex with a raised eyebrow.

"And this is Richard, my Beta."

"It is wonderful to meet you my dear," Richard said, holding his palm out to me. Something inside me screams to not touch it, to stay as far away from this man as I possibly can.

"Hello," I say, keeping my hands in my lap.

Richard frowns, "Why don't you join me for dinner. I would enjoy having your company."

"She is..." Alex begins to say before Richard interrupts him.

"You stay silent and eat your meal."

I watch Alex's arms press into the table, shoving a handful of meat into his mouth with tense muscles.

"Come, I would like to hear about how you met Alex here," Marcus commands, pulling me to my feet.

As we talk away from Alex I feel as if a veil is lifted from in front of me. Suddenly there are dozens of connections open all around me. Three other bridges form instantly just by me looking toward them. Whatever power was blocking me before now seems to be... *Guiding me?*

That same energy pulls my eyes to Richard as we take our seat at a table across the yard.

A fog of black and red oozes out from one of the bridges. I reach for it pulling my hand back as searing pain and terror rips through me. I put up a barrier, carefully reaching out across the bridge, visibly seeing my connection to Alice as memories crash through me in bursts.

I see Alice kneeling before Marcus as she tells him of Richard's rage. His needless slaughtering of a human village. I feel her dread as Marcus commands her to sooth Richard's spirit, *"We need Richard, Alice, he is my hand. Without him, we would be weak."*

The memory fades, the transition jarring me as I am suddenly in a small room. I see Alice holding Mia. Both of them are bloodied and bruised as Richard screams at them. Commanding them to remain silent.

I am thrust back to the present, the same energy shattering the bridge like glass.

I feel dizzy as another surge of power gathers in my mind. Pushing me, forcing me to connect with Marcus and Richard's minds at the same time. Pulling for secrets long buried.

I am standing in a dark forest, a nearly depleted moon overhead. Marcus and Richard look disturbed, nervous even, as they pace.

"Are we really doing this Marcus?" Richard asks.

"We can't turn back now. Just let me do the talking," Marcus says.

The bushes shift. A hooded figure steps into view with a drawn crossbow pointed straight at them. "Two little wolves. Have you come to die?" A female voice asks.

"We came to make a deal," Marcus announces, holding out his hands to either side. "None of us want this slaughter to continue."

The female cackles, "Then why not kill you both and have done with it?"

"Listen," Richard blurts out, stumbling in front of Marcus. "Listen, you know as well as I that you can't kill us all. The Old One will still reincarnate."

A silence grows between them, the woman shifting her feet ever so slightly, "What do you propose?"

Marcus pushes Richard to the side with two fingers. "On the new moon, convince the boy to come out here. We will use him to draw out the Old One. While we fight him, you weaken him with one of those," Marcus says, pointing to the crossbow. "Then we will finish the job."

"How does this help me?"

"We will leave the boy alive, the Old One will transfer to him and I will become Alpha. Once that happens you can tell your root witches that you did it, and I will ensure my small batch of wolves stay tucked away. It will be as if we stopped existing."

"And the boy?"

"I leave that piece of the puzzle to you. Do we have a deal?" Marcus asks, stepping forward and holding out a hand.

The woman pulls back her hood to reveal curly, jet black hair. Their hands clasp, the air becoming thick. As if lighting had struck.

"Deal."

My skin crawls, pulling me back to the present as I feel something wet and rough slide up my neck.

CHAPTER 19

A vile mixture of panic and fury rolls through me, destroying my appetite. Despite this I continue to eat, obeying my Beta's command. The meat tastes like sand in my bloody mouth. My wolf is fighting desperately to rise to the surface, having already transformed our fangs.

"Move!" my wolf roars within me.

My partially shifted fangs tearing into my gums as I grind my teeth, *I can't.*

The remainder of the pack has returned to eating. Their hushed conversations, mere wind compared to my thundering heart.

"You smell nice for an elf," Richard groans.

My wolf snaps at me when Vera doesn't respond.

I will myself to look up, every vein in my neck threatening to burst. Vera's eyes are pitch black as she stairs unemotionally at the food before her. Richard brushes the hair from her neck, his eyes devouring her delicate skin as he leans in closer.

My world stops when his tongue touches her flesh. Everything becomes red as I leap through the air roaring, *"Mine!"*

My clothing shreds into ribbons around me as I crash into Richard. His hands come up, wrestling with my jaws inches from his throat as we collide with the tree behind him, the wood splintering from the impact.

"Oh, little wolf, how I will enjoy crushing you beneath my boot," Richard said, licking his lips. His eyes take on a vibrant yellow. I feel a rush of energy shoot toward me, flowing over me like a gentle breeze. Richard head cocks to the side, confusion rippling across his face.

I push forward, frantically snapping my jaw.

Richard pivots to the right, slamming me against the tree again.

My wolf takes control, his claws digging to the bark of the tree and kicking off as he sinks his front claws into

Richard's chest, bringing him down on the table in an explosion of wood.

"Fucking die!" he shouts. I feel the cold iron enter my side, blood pooling around it without pain. He pulls the blade out, going for another strike.

I lunge, locking my jaw around his throat, tearing it open. His body collapses, blood and guts pouring out around us.

Power surges through me as I take my place as Beta, my focus turning to Marcus.

Marcus' teal eyes shift to a dark amber, his face wrinkling with a mixture of pain and rage. "None of you move!" I feel the wave of his command spread throughout the Pack, each of their eyes suddenly glowing, their bodies stiff as stone. "Per the old laws I let you fight Richard. You can stop here, and keep your life little pup."

"He dies!" my wolf's voice roars within my mind. Charging toward our Alpha.

He flips a table over, the wood slamming against me. My wolf crashes to the ground, a cold air washing over me. The world returns to its normal color, the pack magic vanishes from my veins. Leaving me drained, *weak* as I pant for air, my wolf silent within me.

Marcus lands on my back, wrapping his arm around my throat, lifting me to my hind paws. "You really believed you would kill me. I have been leading this pack since your father died, boy."

I let out a high-pitched snarl, snapping my jaw as I try to turn to face him.

"To think that your root witch hasn't come for you all this time." I feel his grip tighten, choking the air from me, my bones threatening to snap.

Is this how it ends? I think, my legs thrashing just off the ground.

"NO!" Vera's voice pierces through me as she drives a blade through Marcus' side.

Marcus grunts, loosening his grip. I take advantage, twisting upward and willing the shift. My now human legs appear around Marcus' neck. I twist hard, an audible *snap* ripping through the air as we both fall to the ground.

My lungs burn as I gasp for breath. Warmth returns to my skin as my wolf stirs back to life within me. I push myself up onto all fours, crawling to Vera. A sense of relief washing over me as I see her unharmed.

I pull us both to our feet, staring into her beautiful orange eyes.

"Alpha," Alice whispers.

The words echoing from the mouths of each member of the pack as they all take a knee, bowing their heads. I feel the bonds form between each of them. Bits of their strength, their life force flowing along it, feeding into me.

Raw power and need courses through me as I look out over the Pack, *my Pack*. Feeling their concern, their doubts, their *fears*. I am their new alpha, but what does that mean for them?

Vera's hand caresses my cheek, sending waves of heat crashing through me. *"You're hurt,"* her voice whispers in my mind.

I caress her cheek in return, her body trembling beneath my touch. My cock hardens as I feel her cool breath against me. The need to kill or fuck overcoming my common sense.

"Mine," a mixture of both my own and Amarak's voices say in unison.

A grin forms across her delicate lips as she steps into my hold.

"Mia," I call, my eyes still locked on Vera.

"Yes," she answers, appearing in front of us.

"Ensure everyone finishes their meal. I need time with my mate."

My heart is pounding in my ears as I climb the stairs of the mansion. Vera's nails dragging along my chest and back. I can smell the bliss of her arousal build with mine as I carry her into my room, the walls shake as I kick the door closed behind us.

Every muscle tightens in anticipation as I gently set her on the bed, our faces inches apart. My fingers brush through her silky hair, my thumb gliding along her jaw.

I look into the endless void of her eyes, barely contained within the deep sunset orange. A low, vibrating growl builds in my chest as her warm cinnamon and vanilla scent envelops the entire room. My cock twitches, pulsing with need.

I nip at the side of her neck, causing her to gasp as she arches up and into me.

I drag my hands up her leg, the tips of my fingers glide under her leather shirt. Her soft skin sending tingles up my arms, "I need to see you."

She moans, biting her lip. Her fingers digging into my hair.

It takes every ounce of what little control I have left to slowly untie her leathers. Kissing along every inch of newly exposed skin. "You are the most beautiful present to un-wrap," I groan, my tongue dragging between her breasts.

Vera's hands come down, brushing along my stomach as she pushes to untie her pants.

I thread my fingers through hers, slowly shaking my head as I pull them to the side, "I plan to savor every bit of you Little Elf."

A whimper escapes her lips as I kiss my way down her stomach. Her fists gripping the blankets.

I let out a long breath, brushing my nose along her stomach as I untie her pants, kissing along her exposed flesh again. My eyes crinkle, a wide smile growing across my face, "What do we have here," I growl, biting down on the lone freckle just above her left hip.

She gasps, her hips pressing hard against my lips as I lick around a small bruise.

I unlace the final tie, the cutest whimper escaping her lips as she wriggles beneath me. Looking up, I find those beautiful eyes watching me, pleading for me to continue.

I slowly pull her pants down. My nails dragging along her skin as I take a long deep breath, her arousal practically bringing me to my bursting point. "I will never get tired of your scent," I moan.

I reveal her dripping wet slit, desire swirling within me as I eagerly slide my tongue through her sweet nectar. She shrieks, kicking the final bits of her pants off. One of her hands slaps against my head, taking a fist full of hair as she grinds into me.

"More," she pants, her nails digging into my scalp.

Desire unlike anything I have felt before floods through me as I flatten my tongue against her center, devouring my way to her clit. I graze my teeth against the small bundle of nerves, sucking it into my mouth as my tongue swirls around it.

Her thighs slam against my head, squeezing, as her entire body trembles. Her scream, the most magical sound I could imagine.

Her trembling slows as I gently push her thighs apart again. Gliding up to her lips, my cock pulsing as our tongues grapple for dominance. I slide my cock against her sopping pussy. Groaning at the electric sensation shooting from its tip down through my toes as I feel her hot center wrap around me.

She whines, biting down on my lip. Her legs wrap around me again, pulling me deeper. I feel her stretch, heat burning through me as she takes every inch of me.

I slowly pull back, stopping just short of pulling out as I thrust into her again. Our flesh crashing together as her hardened nipples brush against me.

I need this. You. Us.

My heart soars inside of me as I feel my climax building in my core. "I'm..." I choke out, driving my cock deep inside her, roaring with the pleasure of my release.

She screams, her nails tearing into my back. Her pussy clenching around my cock as she spirals into bliss along with me.

The room grows still. My eyes taking in her beauty again, my breath heaving out it bursts.

She rolls me over, keeping my cock firmly locked within her as she threads her fingers into mine. Her hair framing her sparkling eyes as she leans down, kissing me on the cheek before nuzzling into my chest.

"Mine," I sigh, lights dancing around the room as we lay there, locked together.

Chapter 20

My blanket fortress defends us from the outside world. Alex's warmth and scent soothing my nerves as I desperately cling to the peace I have found within his arms.

I still can't believe it... *we had sex.* Despite feeling the safest I have in months, there is a small part of me trembling in fear.

Mine.

He claims me as his, yet something inside me is terrified that he will disappear, leaving me alone within the darkness of my mind.

A mind that was careening over a cliff as I watched Marcus crushing the life from him. Every single one of my fears manifesting in that moment. That I would put him in danger. That he would follow everyone else that chose to be close to me. That he would die trying to protect me.

I reach across the bridge, desperate to know what he is thinking. His mind, a flood of desire that before, was so powerful that my body burned as I ached for his touch. Now it feels more like a gentle stream. Dozens of whispering thoughts that don't belong to him dance along its surface.

Alpha.

That's what they all called him the moment that Marcus' neck snapped. Yet while they all kneeled before him, he never looked away from me. His entire soul aching to be close to mine.

Alex moans, the roughness of his chest brushing against my back. I roll over in his arms. The satisfaction in his sleepy eyes melting my fears away. "Good morning," he rasps with a soft smile.

"Good morning," I mutter, biting my lip as I remember all the places those lips had explored a few hours ago.

His eyes shimmer, traveling down my body, "You smell amazing."

I rest my head against his chest, heat building in my core once again.

JOEY KINCAID

A knock erupts from the door. "Alpha," a hushed voice says. "We need you down stairs."

Alex lets out an exasperated sigh laced with disappointment, "We'll be down in a minute." He rolls over, wrapping a leg around me, purring into my ear, "I love you."

Unable to form those words I wiggle into him, feeling him swell in response.

"Oh," he purrs. "You're going to make me a liar." Sinking his teeth into my shoulder.

I am completely spent as Alex rises from the bed, pulling his pants over his firm ass. My eyes travel up his scarred back, his wide shoulders covered in muscles. I spot the bits of dried blood on his side. Surprised to find the knife wound replaced by smooth pale skin. *Werewolves heal fast*. I think to myself, enjoying the last bits of visible flesh before he covers it with his shirt.

He turns, setting a fresh pair of clothes on the bed. His vibrant blue eyes devouring me as I lay on my stomach. I pet the fur lined blankets as my bare legs dance in the air behind me.

"You take your time Little Elf," he says, his arms bulging as he closes the door behind him.

The room feels terrifyingly empty as he leaves. The cold air is suddenly biting at my skin. I roll under the blankets, our mixed scents surrounding me. Allowing me to hold onto that inner peace for a little longer while taking in the room.

The walls are bare except for the single wall sconce that casts a faint bit of flickering light along the wall. The bed takes up the majority of the room, a small four drawer dresser and stool off to one side under a small frost covered window.

It feels nice, the small space reminding me of home with the added luxury of a window to the outside world. I pull my clothes under the blankets, letting the heat seep into the cold leather, dreading the idea of having to climb out of my personal cocoon of safety.

"You know he won't stick around," my voice bursts from the stool next to the window. I glare at the robed figure of myself. "What? He is a werewolf."

I pull the blanket over my head, desperately trying to find any new connections to my mind.

"You're not going to find anything in there."

"You're not real," I snap. My blood runs cold as I find no strange connections.

She lets out an irritated sigh, "I am just trying to help you. I want you to be safe."

I pull my legs up to my chest, "I am safe."

"You're out of the mines, sure, but with these monsters? No, you are far from safe here."

"He wouldn't hurt me."

She laughs, my bones shivering at the sound. "Look at yourself, he already did."

I lift the blanket up slowly, letting light from the window trickle along my skin. Tiny bruises litter my breasts and stomach. My hand traces along my shoulders, feeling the tender skin heat. "He wasn't..."

"Trying to hurt you?" she cackles, a horrible sound that I can hardly believe is mine. "He wasn't worried about you."

"Shut up," I whisper under my breath, my skin tingling.

"He needed a rut after becoming Alpha, and he took it."

"Shut up," I whisper, tension building in my throat. My breath is visible beneath the covers.

"That's all you are to him. A good hole to fuck."

"Shut up!" I scream, throwing back the blankets. The walls shudder and creak, frost building in the air as the candles barely cling to life. I look to the stool, finding it vacant.

The door crashes open. Slamming against the wall as a large man stumbles in. He takes in the room with wide eyes, rubbing his arms as he puffs out large plumes of white condensation. His lips turning blue, "Are you ok Luna?"

My brows pinch together. *Luna?* I pull the blankets over my bare chest, my heart trying desperately to break free, "I'll be fine."

The man looks around the room again before looking down at me, "When you are ready, Luna, the Beta is making breakfast." Slowly retreating from the room as he pulls the door closed, watching the walls as if expecting them to spring to life at any moment.

Each step creaks as I descend the stairs. The central chandelier provides an inviting glow to the space. I frown at the fact that nearly every window has been shattered and boarded up instead of being replaced. The small gaps allowing the frigid breeze to float in, forming goosebumps along my arms.

Yeah, that needs to be fixed.

The smell and sound of sizzling meat fills the air as I reach the bottom of the stairs. A soothing hum echoing from down the hall. I follow it to find Mia in the kitchen, cooking over a wood burning stove.

I lean against the door frame, closing my eyes. Her humming melts away a tension in my shoulders that I didn't realize I was carrying.

I feel a tug on my shirt and leap into the air with a shriek.

"I scared you!" Lue giggles, looking up at me as her oversized brown sweater sways from side to side.

I rest my hand on my chest, willing my heart to calm back down, "You sure did."

"Who are you?" she asks, cocking her head to the side.

I crouch down to her height, looking into her brown eyes, "My name is Vera. It's nice to officially meet you, Lue."

"Lue, sweety, I need your help," Mia calls.

Lue beams up at me, skipping to her mom and climbing onto a stool.

"How are you feeling?" Mia asks, adding several chopped onions to the sizzling pan.

"Sore," I admit, rubbing the back of my neck. "What are you making?"

Mia's smile brings a glow to her face, "Boar, Ben caught it fresh this morning."

"It smells fantastic."

"Can I go play?" Lue asks, twisting back and forth.

"Sure, but stay in the house. We are going to eat soon," Mia says.

Lue sprints down the hall, disappearing around the corner before Mia finishes her sentence.

"So, do you know how to control it?"

Did the kitchen get smaller? I lean against the wall beside her, "Control what?"

Mia gives me a sideways glance, "He isn't the smartest wolf in the pack, but he knew to tell me what he saw the second he left your room."

I twist the bits of fur sticking out of the bottom of my shirt, "Why did he call you Beta?"

"Because I am the new Beta now," Mia states, glancing back at me. "Will you please answer my question?"

I pick at one of my nails, unsure why I feel guilty. "No... I don't." *Yeah, tell the werewolf that you don't know how to stop yourself from blowing up the house.*

Mia purses her lips, nodding her head slowly. "Okay. Just know that we are here for you. You don't need to try and hide things or solve them on your own. If you need anything just say so."

"Why?" I ask, my mouth hanging open as I reach out, touching her mind.

"You're family now. We look out for our family." She pulls the pan off the stove, spooning its contents between three plates.

Family? I feel my chest tighten at the trust behind those words. A small hand wrapping around my finger.

"It's okay. Mommy's food is really good," Lue says, her smile taking up her entire face. I wipe away a tear before it trails down my cheek, forcing a smile to my face.

"Thank you."

The air feels sharp against my skin as I step outside. The snow has melted away, leaving the ground muddy. The trees creak with the wind as beams of sunlight peak through the thick canopy.

"Alice. That is enough," Alex commands from the center of the backyard.

Several of the tables are still overturned while others are completely destroyed.

Alice's chest puffs out as she steps right into Alex's face, a finger inches from his nose as she glares into his eyes. "No. You listen," she demands, mimicking Alex's tone.

Lue grips my leg, hiding most of her body behind me as Mia slowly moves toward them.

What is happening? I reach for my connection with Alice.

Alice's eyes flick to mine the moment I make the connection, her shimmering jade eyes shooting darts at me as she spears a finger in my direction, "Her kind are the *reason* that the human kingdom fell. They are why *we* are forced to live like this."

Her voice screams anger and fury, but her mind shows the truth. *Alice is hurting.* The wounds of hidden pain and betrayal from years of abuse now bleeding freely within her.

Alex's eyes ignite, the air becoming thick with heat. The veins on his arms and throat threatening to burst through his skin. His voice, a guttural warning, "Alice."

A tortuous echo builds within Alice's mind as her wolf lets out a snarling whimper, desperate to fight and run all at the same time.

Alice's face crinkles, her eyes burning with rage. "Just because she gets you hard doesn't mean she deserves our protection."

Alex lets out a roar, his fist ripping through the air. Mia appears between them. Her palm slaps against his forearm. The relatively small move causes his fist to graze through

Alice's hair instead of crashing into her face. Alice stumbles back, her eyes wide.

"Don't move!" Mia barks at Alice before locking eyes with Alex. She holds her gaze, beads of sweat pouring down her face. Appearing to be in physical pain before looking to the ground. "Alex, *Alpha*, you chose me for a reason. Please, let me handle this." Her eyes flicking back to me and Lue.

Alex follows her gaze, his eyes fixing on me. His face slowly relaxes. His fangs retract as his eyes fill with concern, fear, *dread*.

I push out for my bridges to his mind. Where I expect to find the twin bridges of stone and roots, I instead am met with a sheer wall of pitch-black obsidian, its surface as cold as ice.

Alex closes his eyes, taking a deep breath as he looks back to Mia, keeping his voice low, "Very well."

Mia turns completely around, her shoulders tight as she regards Alice who has managed to pull her face back to the mask of anger once more. "What is really bothering you, Alice?" Mia asks, peering deep into her eyes.

"She is *our* problem," Alice answers, her fingering shooting toward me again. I can feel both her eyes and that of her wolf lock onto me, feeling the safety it brings her in blaming me for her agony.

"Why?" Mia asks, her head tilting to the side.

"Why?" Alice shouts back. Another wave of pain flooding through her mind. "She carries the shadow of death with her!"

My entire world slows at those words, the bodies of everyone that have died appearing all around me. Their glazed eyes watching me, *judging* me. *So many have died so that I can live.*

My ghosts fade away with a gust of wind. "I agree," my whisper bringing a deafening silence upon the backyard.

"You... what?" For a moment I can almost swear I smell the ocean breeze kicking off the Everenthia cliffside.

"I shouldn't stay here. It isn't fair for me to put you all in harm's way." I look deep into Alice's eyes, feeling her internal struggle. *"They would understand if you told them,"* my words echo through her mind.

"I..." Alice abruptly turns, her words caught in her throat. "Then leave," she huffs, storming into the woods.

Mia lets out a long sigh, dragging a hand through her hair. "I will go talk to her."

Alex flexes his hands as he walks over to me. "Is that really what you want?" he asks, his eyes filled with concern.

I reach out for his bridge, but the wall of obsidian is still in place. *Does he even know he is doing that?*

I feel a shiver rush down my spine, every one of my hairs standing on end as a serpentine voice whispers in my ear, *"Yes."* I look around, searching for the source only to see nothing, *feel* nothing.

"Vera?" Alex asks, touching my shoulder.

I look to the ground, a part of me wants to tell him. To tell him how I am seeing, hearing, even arguing with myself. If that wasn't bad enough, now I am hearing strange voices that aren't even real. *He would think I was crazy if I told him.* "Yes. At least until the elves stop their search."

"Okay, then you can come with me," Alex concedes, gently guiding my face back up to his. "You never need to feel guilty for what you want."

I force a smile to my face, "Right."

"Besides, it has been far too long since I have gone home."

CHAPTER 21

The sun has been beating down on us for the last few days as we continue down the road to Red River. The snow long since melted away, allowing the fresh smell of the forest to float through the air.

I have been watching Vera closely since we left. She has been quiet, her eyes focusing on open areas, just a tang of fear tainting her tranquil scent. I've tried to ask her what's wrong, but she just tells me, *"I'll be okay."* It's not a lie, but I can feel it. Something is wrong. She just won't tell me what it is.

Even my wolf is getting restless, our evenings filled with sprinting out into a wide patrol every night after Vera falls asleep. Yet every night it's the same, we can smell our own intertwined scents in the air. Maybe a few animals here and there, but nothing else. Not even a hint of something tailing us. *So, what has her so scared?*

"Alex?" Vera asks, her beautiful orange eyes sending waves of warmth through me. "Can we take a break?"

"Of course," I say, spotting the perfect fallen tree just up the road for a rest. "Let's just get over there and we can stop for lunch."

"That sounds good," she replies, looking back the way we came. I look down the path, my wolf eyes seeing nothing but a rabbit hop across the trail. Vera hugs my arm, leaning on me as we start to walk again.

Despite not knowing why she is nervous. I can't help the pride that fills me as she takes comfort in our closeness, her heart fluttering every time my wolf purrs. *I would carry you the entire way, if only to feel your soft skin.*

"Do you think we will be there soon?"

I take a deep breath, the smell of fresh cut lumber and river moss tickling my nose. "Yeah. I can smell the lumber yard. We will probably be there by mid sun."

She eases herself onto the log, rotating her feet in the air with a groan. "Good, I don't know if I can take another day of walking."

"Here," I offer, kneeling between her legs. I watch her cheeks turn red as my hand cups her calf, holding her foot in the air as I slide her boot free. Revealing her small, smooth feet.

"What are you..." Her voice trailing off as I begin working her foot. "Ohhh. Okay, yeah, we can do that."

I attack each of the tiny knots with practiced hands, appreciating how soft even her feet are. I drop my face slightly, remembering all the times I did this for Altha. How Ben had said she went missing. *Would the village have searched for her? Helped her?* They never seemed to care before. Unless of course *they* needed something.

"What is it?" Vera asks, her gentle voice pulling me to the present.

"I used to massage Altha's feet."

"Your teacher?"

"Yeah. She would always get grouchy after the snow began to melt and I would need to massage away the swelling." I can't help the chuckle that escapes my lips. Hearing Altha's voice play in my head, tell me to not press so hard, only to demand that I press harder a few moments later.

"It sounds like you were close."

"She raised me. After my mom..." My words trail off, the memory from Vera's mind flashing before me again. "When *Claire* left."

I return my focus on her feet, working a stubborn knot just under her toes. I don't need to look in her eyes to know the pain that lingers there. She may have unintentionally shone me Claire's death, but that woman was closer to Vera than she had ever been to me. After Dad died, she couldn't even look at me. Altha was the one that stood beside me through the pain, the sleepless nights, the endless tears. Altha gave me something to hold on to. She gave me a purpose, when I had nothing else.

"She loved you," Vera says, barely above a whisper.

She loved the idea of me. "I just hope Altha is okay. The last thing I heard from Ben was that she was missing." Finally feeling satisfied with the first foot I slide her boot back on and move to the next one.

"If you knew that, why didn't you go back sooner?"

"I couldn't. Richard had forbidden me from returning." My eyes narrow, remembering how easily we took him down. If only I had been stronger, not so afraid, maybe I could have left to help her sooner.

"Why did you listen to him? Why did any of you?"

I can feel Vera's muscles relax as I work the last few knots out of her other foot, even as I watch her shoulders and face tighten. "When a more dominant wolf commands another, your entire body reacts. Not your mind. If you fight the command... it feels like the air itself is trying to crush you."

Vera sighs, leaning back as I dig into the last stubborn knot. "Well, at least you can finally see your home again."

My head begins to throb just at the idea of stepping foot there again. It feels like years have gone by since Mike, Ben and Todd attacked me. Tossing me into that cart with the hope that I would never return. Of course, it's hard to be mad at them when that led me to her, to my mate.

A grin tugs at my lips as my eyes travel up Vera's leg, the urge to devour every inch of her building within me. "Truthfully, home is wherever you are."

My hand moves up the back of her calf, small bumps forming along her skin. "Alex," she moans, her fingers wrapping around mine.

"Yes?" I slowly crawl up to her, our bodies inches apart. The sweet smell of her arousal building.

"Wa... wait."

My nose grazes up the elegant slope of her neck as I gently draw circles with my tongue.

Her hands press against my chest. "Wait," she bites out.

My heart is pounding in my chest as I pull back. A fire roars within me as I find her gaze looking behind me, fear rippling across her face.

I press off the rock, my fangs pushing out, prepared to rip apart whatever it is. Only to find... *nothing?* I smell only the forest mixed with our scent. My wolf scans the forest, detecting no movement.

I turn back to Vera, finding her pulling her jacket tight over herself, her face tight, eyes locked on the earth. My face drops, feeling as if someone had just dumped a tub of ice water over me. *Me?*

"Did I?" The words catch in my throat.

"Can we go?" she whispers, not even glancing in my direction.

"Of... of course," I push out, moving to slide her boot back on. She grabs it instead, putting it on herself before standing and continuing down the path.

My wolf begins to circle in my mind, his concern only doubling my own as I grab our bags and follow our mate. *Whatever I have done, I need to fix it.*

Music fills the air as the village comes into view. Bursts of shouts and laughter muddying the otherwise beautiful songs.

"I wonder what they are celebrating," Vera says, her voice once again filled with warmth.

It's the first thing she's said since we started moving again. Every one of my muscles feel tight and heavy, picking apart what happened on that tree.

I can smell the stench of vomit and alcohol from here. The thought of George breaking out enough alcohol for it to carry this far along the wind tells me that either someone is visiting that has a lot of money, or the celebration is for him.

"Must be something big. George broke out the ale," I say, forcing a warmth I don't feel into my voice.

"George?"

"He owns the lumber mill, the tavern *and* the store." I flex my hands, the need to punch something only compounding with time. Her heartbeat has slowed and she is more relaxed. She has moved forward from whatever happened. *Why can't I?*

"So, he is the Lord of Red River then?" she asked.

"He would agree with you, but no. The human lands don't have any lords, we live on land owned by the other races, at their discretion."

She stops, her brows pinching together, "Really? Then who leads them?"

"The elders of the town talk it over and come to an agreement. Sure, George might control the primary source of work and trade within the village, but at the end of the day everyone is their own person."

"I like that," she says, her teeth peeking out through her smile. She holds her hand out to me, "Shall we?"

The path before us will lead right to the square. I swallow hard, taking her hand in mine. No longer concerned with what will happen here. *I would follow you into the depths of the Great Tear if you asked.*

The square is filled with people dressed in their finest clothes as they dance and cheer. White fabric is twisted and hung between houses. Each of the braziers popping and crackling with fire that battles away the chill of the impending night. Large tables overflow with food as children snatch bits of it before sprinting away with laughter.

Paula, perched upon a balcony overlooking the square is playing a shanty that fills the space with contagious joy.

Vera's hand grips mine hard as she lets out a hiss, slapping her other hand against her forehead.

"Are you okay?" I ask.

"Yeah," she grunts, her eyes squinting as she looks back into the crowd. "Yeah, I'm okay. It's just been a while since I have been around so many people."

"We can leave." *Please, let us leave.*

"No. No, this is nice. We don't have music like this in Everenthia."

"I would be happy to…"

A high-pitched squeal erupts from the crowd as a woman dressed in all white rushes forward, her golden hair flowing with the wind.

Emily?

She leaps into the air, crashing into me full force. I stumble back, catching her just as I bump into a table sending several plates clattering to the ground. Her signature overpowering rose scented perfume enveloping me. *Yep... that's Emily.*

"I can't believe you're here!" Emily squeals, my ears still ringing from her first assault.

I glance between Emily and Vera, my mouth wide as I finally catch my bearings, "Emily." I carefully lower her back to the ground. The elegant fabric of her dress glinting off the faint light. "It's great to see you too, you look beautiful."

Her chin nearly touches her chest, her smile widening, "Ah, thank you. Daddy had it made special for today. Did you get Mike's letter? Oh, what am I saying, of course you did. Why else would you be here."

"We didn't get any letters from Mike," Vera says, stepping beside me and gripping my arm.

Emily launches a single eyebrow into the air as she looks her up and down, "Well Alex, are you going to introduce us?"

I cough, my eyes darting around. "Vera this is Emily Mills, she..."

"Barret," Emily interrupts.

"W... What?" I stutter, my head beginning to throb.

"Emily Barret, Mike and I just got married," she informs, presenting the intricate runic pattern drawn on her arms.

"Congratulations," Vera offers, bowing her head slightly as she loosens her grip on my arm.

"Yes," I say, my face pinching together. *Mike? You married Mike?* "Anyway, she is the daughter of George Mills. Emily, this is Vera..." My voice trails off. *I don't even know her last name...*

"It's nice to meet you Emily," Vera says, shaking her hand.

"Alex. My cup is empty," Emily says, holding out the cup that reeks of wine. "Would you be a dear and fill it up while I get to know Vera here a little more?"

I look at Vera, "I don't know if..."

"Go on, can you get me one too please?" Vera asks, her lips pulling into a shallow smile.

You sure? I say with my eyes before grabbing her cup, "You got it."

I feel like I am trudging through a river with each step. Continually looking back as I push through the crowd, getting glimpses of Emily laughing at whatever Vera just said. *Emily and Vera seem to be getting along at least.*

My wolf begins to pace within my mind, his unease threatening my already thin self-control. *I know buddy, I will hurry up.*

I finally reach the wine table, frowning at the intricately carved fountain of the happy couple. Wine continuously flowing on a loop through it. I hold my breath, dunking Emily's cup into the foul liquid. *How does anyone drink this?*

"Alex!" a drunken voice booms from behind me. I turn to find Mike, his black formal wear slightly wet with, presumably, what is splashing from the large stein in his hand as he stumbles toward me.

"Mike," I say, not even attempting to hide the anger in my eyes.

"I thought I told you to not come back," he slurs, shoving his stein into the wine and instantly taking a drink of it.

"I see you haven't changed," I venture, carefully setting Emily's cup on the table.

Mike rests against the table, looking toward Vera and Emily, "Ah yeah? Well I *won*," Mike says, punching his stein toward them causing some of the wine to splash onto the ground.

"I am happy for you both," I lie, gently placing a hand on his shoulder. "I think you have had enough, Mike."

"Shhhh. Can I axe you somthin'?" Mike asks, gripping my shirt, his grin stretching the width of his face.

"How'd you get the elven whore?"

I no longer hear the music playing. The dancing crowd drops away as I glare down at him. My knuckles crack, nails digging into my palms.

He reaches down, gripping his crotch, chuckling, "I'd like some of that."

It happens in a flash, a blur of color as my world flashes red just before my fist crushes into his face. My wolf steps in, the world fading to blue as that same hand wraps around his throat. Lifting him into the air before slamming him back down through the table.

Shrieks echo from behind me as wine floods over him. I throw the fountain to the side, revealing his bloodied face. My canines protrude over my lips as I continue to pummel into him. My fists come back bloodier each time.

Several burly arms wrap around me, throwing me off of him in unison. The largest of the four shouts words I can't make out over the pounding in my ears as I roll to my feet, preparing to charge them as well.

Just as I step forward to swing, Vera's scream scorches down my spine. I spin around, the men behind me vanishing from my world all together. My jaw slowly drops, my eyes opening wide, yet only able to see one thing.

Vera?

Chapter 22

"That is a wonderful dress," I compliment, watching Alex push through the crowd. My head feels ready to explode, every mind in the square slamming against the barriers I put in place when we arrived.

"You are too kind," Emily says, gliding her hands along the fabric. "Though I am sure you have seen far more glamorous dresses in the elven kingdom."

I force out a laugh. *Hopefully the wine will help numb my mind.* "That does not make your gown any less beautiful. Are any of your family here?"

Emily begins to talk but her words become background noise to the barrage of voices flooding through a crack in my walls.

"I can't believe he brought an elf here."

"He was always weird."

"Emily is talking with it."

I quickly seal the gap, each of the minds pounding harder than before. *I don't understand, it has never been this hard before.*

"Why not let them in?" a serpent-like voice whispers in my ear.

I launch to my feet, turning to find the space empty, excluding Emily who is now frowning at me.

"Did I say something to offend?" she asks.

"No... no, I thought I heard something." My head throbs again, bringing me to my knees. "Ah, it hurts," I hiss.

Emilys rests her hand on my shoulder, "Vera?"

A dark, cold feeling trickles across my mind. *"Let's let them in,"* the voice slithers. I feel the barriers crack and splinter, the voices stampeding through my mind. Their every thought an open book.

"Is she ok?"

"It's a trick to demand more lumber."

"Never trust an elf."

I feel my skin heat. Someone beside me gasps as they stumble away. "Stop!" I scream, clawing at the sides of my head, squeezing my eyes shut.

"She hurt Emily!"

"She's a witch!"

"Protect the children!"

The world vanishes, replaced by the hurricane within my mind. The voices echoing, building into a sound that ravages its way through me. I feel blood drip from my nose, my teeth grinding, my throat going horse.

"Vera!" a muffled voice yells.

I open my eyes, seeing only a swirling vortex of darkness and blue flame. The voices swirling around me, screaming at me in pain, fear, *terror*.

"Stop!" I scream again, attempting to throw up my walls. They instantly shatter like glass only adding to the swirling darkness around me.

"Vera!" the voice yells again, a hand erupting from the darkness, glass tearing through it, adding a stream of crimson to the darkness.

I reach for it, my muscles igniting with a pain that forces me back to the ground.

I feel two hands lock around my face, pulling my eyes up. "Vera! Look at me!" Alex's glowing blue eyes envelop me like a warm blanket, silencing the world around me.

I scramble into the safety of his arms, my blood burning within my veins.

"I'm here," he gasps, squeezing me tight. "I've got you." Those words, his voice, his presence finally allows my mind to drift to sleep.

My entire body feels as though it was trampled by a crowd as I push myself up from the soft blankets. A small fire crackles beside me under a large black cauldron. The warm light dancing along the worn wooden walls around me.

I reach for the table, pulling myself to my feet as I take in the space. The cabinet doors in the kitchen hang precariously from their hinges, random bits of moldy food and shattered jars are scattered about the counter. I follow my nose to the cauldron, discovering a red soupy mixture that smells of tomatoes and herbs.

My stomach rumbles as I continue to look around the room. My eyes come to rest on Alex. He is resting in a small white rocking chair that is probably better suited for someone half his size. The faintest bit of moonlight glistening off his skin.

I will my legs forward, tensing at the stabbing pain in my calves. I hold back a gasp, finally able to see Alex, his entire chest and arms covered in bandages. *Did I?*

"Yes, you did that," my voice bursts from the kitchen. I turn to find the robbed version of me leaning against the counter.

I look between Alex and her, fumbling for my words, "I... that... It wasn't my fault. I didn't mean to."

"Yet you did, and look at him."

I crouch to the floor, snatching up a chunk of wood and hurl it through the air. It flies through her, clattering along the floor as a bone chilling cold runs through me. "No..." I whisper as the last bit of air leaves my lungs.

"What? You have been saying I'm not real for so long. Yet now you are shocked?"

The room spins around me, "I'm going crazy."

The image of myself cackles, a horrendous sound that rattles my bones. "Going? Look at him. Will you really force him to be the next one to die for you?"

Alex's breathing is shallow, his rising chest barely visible. "You were wrong about him." My eyes shooting daggers back at the image.

"Yes, I will admit. I was wrong before. He has proven that he would die for you. Then again, is that really what you want? Another corpse at your feet?"

I follow its gesture, stumbling back as I gasp for air. Blood covers his entire body. Pools of it gathering on the floor, large shards of glass protruding from every inch of his body. "No!" I scream, crashing to the floor. I reach for his bridge, refusing for it to be real.

She is fake, this must be fake!

The cold obsidian wall greats me. My fists slamming against it as I scream again and again.

"Look at him again," she says, pulling me back.

My screams quiet as I use the wall to stand once more, tears flowing down my cheeks. The blood is gone, his breathing shallow but still present, "Why would you show me that?"

"You need to understand what will happen if you stay with him. Today you hurt him. *You* hurt him. What about tomorrow? A week from now? You're poison to him."

I walk to his side, my hand caressing his rough skin. My fingers tingling from his warmth. "You're right," I say, leaning down and gently kissing his cheek. "I can't stay."

I grab my things, smiling at how his scent still clings to the jacket. "Goodbye," I whisper, stepping out the front door.

The darkness in the yard envelops me, the moon barely a sliver.

Tomorrow will be new moon.

I shiver at the bitter cold, pulling my jacket close just as something latches around my throat. My hands shoot up, gripping the leather collar now scorching against my skin.

Black scaled arms wrap around me, lifting me into the air and covering my mouth. "Thank you so much for leaving..." my own voice whispers in my ear. "That wretched women's house," the serpent-like voice finishes.

It leans in, rubbing its scales against my skin as it takes a long inhale, black ooze lingers in its wake. "Your power will be so delicious."

CHAPTER 23

"Where is she?" I scream, sweat dripping from every inch of my body. I can still taste the bitterness of it, the Nitpaw that must have lined the cauldron nearly put me to my knees. How long had she been infusing our food, was it not enough for me to drink it daily?

Her scent is faint, maybe eight hours old, but there is nothing else. *Why would she leave?* I storm for the front door, nearly ripping it from its hinges as it slams against the wall. It's then that it hits me. The overpowering stench of sulfur and rot.

"Demon," my wolf growls. My canines cut into my gums with their sudden growth.

"We need to..."

"Wait," an old voice vibrates behind me. A large figure, cloaked in shadow appears in front of me. Its red and yellow eyes along with its needle-like teeth piercing through its veil of darkness. "Listen," it commands, presenting a small bench with its twisted obsidian talon.

It smells of dirt, moss and *old* magics. "What have you done with her?" I ask, my arms burning with power, desperate to be put to purpose.

"Nothing," it says through a heavy breath that reeks of rot.

My wolf rages, taking the reins as we burst forward, ready to tackle it to the ground. It disappears into a cloud of black smoke, forcing me to shift my momentum into a roll. Spotting the figure gazing down at me from where I had been.

"Where is she?" I scream, charging at it again.

"Stop." The command vibrates within me as it points its taloned hand to my chest. My legs lock, forcing me to fall on all fours. It feels like gravity is pushing me to the ground as I strain to look up. A map gently falling to the ground before me. Its talon taps a point, black smoke rising from the parchment as an X forms over a clearing just beneath the Great Tear. "There."

My nose crinkles as I meet its gaze, "Vera is there?"

It blinks, nodding its head slowly. "Hurry," it says, vanishing again with a flash of smoke. The weight of the world disappears with it.

I snatch the map up, rising to my feet.

"Demons," my wolf snarls.

"We will need help," I say, rolling up the map and stepping back into Altha's hut.

It is strange, feeling the Pack approach. Even before I smell them, I know they are there. Watching as I walk with purpose through the forest. The wind whispering through the trees as I pass.

This is *mine. My* home. *My* Pack. *My responsibility*.

"Gather in the yard," I command, my voice pushing through the air with finality. I hear the scouts begin to retreat.

My words carry a weight now. A weight that I will not take lightly.

I flex my hands, loosening my arms as I approach the mansion. The fountain with a riderless horse looking down at me as I pass.

To think, just a few months ago I came here terrified. Terrified that if I didn't say or do the right thing, at the right time. If I didn't put on the mask that was expected of me. That I would become that sniveling boy again. Trapped under that tree.

Little did I know that I had never left. Watching the shadows stalk around me as I cowered, desperate for someone to save me, but unable to scream.

Now I am what stalks within the shadows. I am the one that causes others to cower, and I am done waiting.

The yard comes into view, my Pack all sitting in their usual spots. Mia, petting her daughter's hair. Ben picking at his nails. Alice, looking down her nose at me.

"What is it that you want?" Alice snaps. I can feel the emotions of the Pack flow with her words. The ripple of fear that it brings.

"I need your help. Vera was taken by a demon last night."

"A demon? And we should jump to fight, just because you say so?"

I glance at her with a half laugh, "You never really liked me did you Alice?"

"It isn't about me liking you. You became our Alpha, and then left with your Little Elf pet. Now you return to us and want our help retrieving it?"

My eyes ignite blue as I look down my nose at Alice, "You will stop disrespecting my mate."

"That doesn't work on me. Or have you forgotten that I am not here for you? I am here for them," Alice says, spreading her arms wide. "You abandoned them, you chose *her* over them."

I look to the crowd, most of their eyes to the ground, "Is that how you all feel?" I ask them. "That I abandoned you?"

The silence is deafening. My heartbeat thumping in my ears.

"You did leave," Lue says from Mia's lap. Her eyes were wet with tears.

"I did. I did leave, but I didn't leave you alone. I left you with the one person that I would trust to protect you, to guide you," I say, holding my hand out to Mia. Her pride building as she pulls back her shoulders. "I left you Alice, your caretaker that has never asked for anything in return. Even when others take far more than they should."

Alice's eyes look to the ground, pain shooting across her face for an instant.

"I will not stand here and pretend that I know what it means to be Alpha. Because I don't. I don't even know what it means to lead, let alone lead so many. Yet here I stand, before you." I look them all in the eye, one by one, knowing them. Their pain, their joy, their grief. "I am not Marcus. I am not Richard. I will not have you follow me simply because I bested them. I would instead ask that you help me. Help me build a future where we no longer need to hide in the woods. So we don't have to live in a run-down mansion on its last legs. Help me ensure that our children do not have to live in fear of the world. Werewolves were once the guardians of the human empire. We were the ones that put fear into the hearts of our enemies, the ones that pushed back the swarms of demons when everyone else ran." I pause, taking a shallow breath as my eyes plead with each of them. "Vera is not just *my* mate. She is your Luna, and without even knowing what that means, she put you all before herself. Choosing to leave, rather than put you in danger. Again, I won't force you, but I will ask. Who will help me bring our Luna home?"

The sound of uneasy feet shuffle through the dirt as they look to each other for guidance.

"I will," Mia says, rising to her feet.

"Me too," Ben says.

"I won't leave her," another says, my Pack rising to their feet as they join the call.

Alice slowly walks through the crowd to me, all eyes watching her. "When you put it like that, it would be wrong of me to stay."

The crowd roars behind her, their hearts beating with focused power.

"Let's bring her home!"

Chapter 24

My muscles ache from continually fighting, blood dripping from where I cut myself against my captor's black scales. The purest of darkness floods the land around us, the new moon holding back even the faintest hope of light as I watch the forests move farther and farther away.

He had ripped my jacket, binding my hands and feet with it before finally gagging my mouth. The cold is nipping at me through my thin shirt.

"Stay here," my captor demands, shrugging me off his shoulder. I crash to the stone covered surface. My head bouncing against it as I grunt in pain.

I try to roll to my back, feeling the jagged stone tear through my shirt. *Obsidian? But obsidian only forms in...*

"The Great Tear? Yes," it says, its serpent tung slithering out of its mouth. It grips my hair, pulling me to a seated position.

My eyes go wide, taking in the pitch-black abyss of the Great Tear.

"Today my dear, you are going to perform a great service."

My jaw clamps down on the gag as I glare through its back.

It turns to me, hundreds of sharp teeth smiling back at me. It disperses into a black mist, appearing inches from my face, one of its hands gripping my hair. "Your bloodline made this barrier," it says, dragging its talon down my cheek, blood trailing along its path. "Your blood will unmake it." It raises its talon over its mouth, letting droplets of my blood land on its tongue, shrieking with delight.

My bloodline?

"Yes my dear. Did you really believe that just anyone could be born a Mindblade? That it was chance?" Its smile grows, taking up nearly its entire face. "No, that gift was granted to the Old One of the elves. Her bloodline. Your, bloodline. To believe that your people would abuse such a wonderful gift."

You're wrong.

It hisses, rushing down at me, its face inches from mine as it rips the gag free, "You have the Old One's blood. The humans were given the ability to shift, the orcs to forge magical items, the fairies foretelling and finally the elves were granted the ability to manipulate the mind."

"If I am so special, why can you do it?" I spit.

It frowns, wiping the spit from its eye. "Simple," it says. Its voice guttural and cold as it glares down at me. "I consumed your mother's heart."

My mental guard slips in that moment, a woman's scream echoing through my mind.

The ground beneath me vanishes as I plummet into the darkness of my own mind, talons wrap around me.

"I'm not the scared little girl anymore!" I scream, twisting out of its hold.

"Is that so?" Its grin widens as it grows to the size of a mountain within my mind. Scooping me into its hand as it drags a talion along the obsidian wall that had blocked my bridge to Alex and Amarak. "I think I have kept this locked away long enough, don't you?"

"It was you?" I hiss, squirming within its hand.

It's talons inches from the wall's surface, "Yes."

"What are you?"

Its eyes shimmer as it looks down at me, "A very old demon my dear. One that is oh so bored." Its talon pushes into the stone, the wall rippling, disintegrating to ash under his touch.

I reach out with my mind, pushing for their connections. I feel them. Their pain, their rage, their need to be near me boiling across it.

"Vera?" Alex's voice echoes through my mind.

I push out to respond but tethers of power wrap around my limbs, holding me in place.

"Now, now, we can't have you ruining all our fun so soon. I did not take this down for you to use my dear. I took it down so that we could play."

My heart goes cold, watching my hands move on their own, hovering over the bridge. "No," I cry out. "Please don't!"

It laughs, the sound crawling over my skin as my hands begin to glow. My eyes bulging, tears flowing down my face as I watch stone after stone lift from the bridge. Disintegrate to dust as the wind carries it into the void. "No! Please stop!" My heart grows cold, feeling the connection shake. Alex's fear doubles as our connection finally shatters, the bridge collapsing into the void completely. I scream, my heart shattering right along with it.

The demon's laugh builds as if feeding off my pain, reveling in my misery.

I grit my teeth, my face wrinkling with rage, "I'll kill you!" Shooting daggers at him with my mind.

He hisses, slapping the daggers that formed out of thin air to the side. "Interesting," it hisses, its grim smile still on its face. "You still have fight left. I have been poking around in that little mind of yours for some time dear. The only reason you made it out of the mine was because of that mutt's bridge. Shall we see how you do without it?"

Its arm grows impossible large, gripping at the walls of my mind. "You really shouldn't put all of these in one place." It pulls hard, memories bursting through, crashing around me.

My skin goes pale, staring down at the rapids of my mind.

"I think I will leave you with these," the demon bellows, sealing me in an obsidian box before dumping me into the rapids below.

What feels like an eternity passes, the memories slamming against the box. Screaming to get to me. I cover my ears, trying to block out their howls. The walls begin to crack, memories squeezing in.

"No!" I scream, pushing myself against the opposite wall.

"Stupid girl!" Morvina shrieks into my ear, her nails digging into my shoulder.

I pull hard, scrambling to the opposite wall.

"I see you need to be broken," the Warden's voice grunts from behind me.

"No!" I roll to the other side, my eyes darting between the two of them.

"It's your fault," my own voice echoes through me, materializing through the wall in front of me.

"No. No I didn't. I..." I close my eyes, my hands tearing into my hair as I plead for them to go away.

"Vera," a warm voice whispers. The memories fading as a familiar soothing warmth washes over me.

I slowly open my hands, looking up to see a tall man sitting in a rocking chair. His sad blue eyes watching me.

"Jack?" I ask, my breath freezing in the throat. The memories slamming against a tornado of shadow and light. "How are you..."

"Pack magic doesn't come from nothing," his words wrap around me, warming my soul. "We live on, in the hearts of those we leave behind. Through our connection we help guide them, even protect them at times."

A memory of the Warden slams against the barrier.

"Go away!" I scream.

Jack leans forward, lacing his fingers together. "They won't," he says, gently shaking his head. "You can't keep running from them either. They are a part of you, whether you like it or not."

Tears well in my eyes, "Why?"

"If you fight the past, you are too tired, too weak to enjoy the present. If you instead choose to embrace the past, accept it for what it is. Then, and only then, can you gain the strength that comes from having survived it."

"What if I can't?" I ask, wiping the tears from my face.

Jack smiles back at me, "You can. You've always been able to." He gets up, walking towards the twirling vortex of shadow and light.

"Wait!" I shout.

Jack stops, looking back at me over his shoulder.

"Is she with you?"

"I have always been with her, and she with me," he says, his form merging with the shadows.

The memories twist and snarl at me, slamming against the barrier in force. I stand, taking a long deep breath.

"I can do this," I whisper, my voice shaky as I step forward. The vortex cracking just enough for memories to leak through. "They are a part of me." I look up, raising my arms up.

The Warden rushes toward me, screaming.

"It happened," I say, the Warden slamming into me, his body becoming mist around me, floating to the ground.

"Stupid girl!" Morvina shrieked, storming toward me.

"I survived it," I whisper. Morvina's hand slaps against my face with no force, her form dissipating into mist around me.

"You don't deserve them!" my own form yells, rushing for me.

I hold out my arms, "I am stronger because of it." As she tackles into me, I wrap my arms around her. Holding her close as she dissipates as well.

My world stills as I open my eyes, the calm silence that I have not felt in months surrounds me. I look towards where the bridges of stone and vines once were. The space is a mere echo of its former self.

I drop to my knees, taking one of the stone blocks into my hands, "I love you."

A single tear flows down my cheek, falling to the ground. Its sound ripples throughout my mind. I look down, just as a single rose sprouts forth, its lush red petals glinting with light.

"I vow to be deserving of your love, from this day, until the end of my days," Amarak and Alex's voices say as one, their energies vibrating through me.

My mindscape fades away, the obsidian landscape surrounding me once more.

I look up toward the demon as it hisses at a shadow, "It didn't work Ogroz. You said that if I merged her blood with the spell that it would fall. The barrier is still there!"

The shadow shifts, pointing to me before dissipating.

"Interesting," the demons shrieks. "How did you break out, I wonder."

I remain silent, feeling for the threads of the demon's connection, for a way to strike back. The collar around my neck burning at the attempt.

The demon lurches forward, licking the side of my neck. It shrieks back, its tongue sizzling as it covers its mouth. "You tarnish your gift with their filth!"

I can hurt you. A grin tugging at my cheeks as the connection between Alex and myself grows stronger. Not a bridge, something more, a *bond*.

The demon's nose pinches tight as it appears in front of me once more, its talons locking around my throat, "What are you smiling about?"

Howls erupt from all around us, filling the night sky as the demon's eyes peer out around us.

Skeletal bones rise from the ground. Shadows swirling around them, through them, manipulating their movements.

My wolves shred through them. Bones scattering throughout the field, only to be gathered by the shadows once more. I charge past them, following my connection to Vera. I don't know how it happened, but our bond has finally formed. I will not lose her now. Not when I finally have her.

The ground trembles, the earth before me jutting up. I tumble back on all fours, my wolf finding his footing easily as we watch the half-rotted remains of a giant emerge from the ground.

It roars, the action sending gusts of wind blasting past us.

My wolf raises its head, howling to the sky. Our Pack joins us, bounding towards the giant. Mia's wolf leaps, climbing along its arm until she reaches its head. Ripping her claws across its throat and down its back until she lands on the ground once more.

If we are to kill the giant, we must kill the one manipulating it.

My wolf charges between its legs, rushing towards the Great Tear. *"The one that holds our mate,"* My wolf growls.

We narrowly dodge the giant's hand. The ground around us jutting up in every direction. Multiple wolves climb its legs, following Mia's example as they claw their way up its body.

As we finally get past it, we hear a whimper, feeling one of our wolves go limp.

A savage snarl erupts from Mia's wolf, as she claws her way up the side of the giant. Digging her claws in with each step. A small wolf on the ground beneath her, unmoving as the giant stumbles.

My wolf snarls, leaving the giant to our Pack as we bound for the demon.

Skeletal hands burst from the ground, grabbing at our legs. We barely slip past, weaving to avoid them.

"Welcome!" the demon shouts, its voice searing into my mind. Stepping into view as it drags our mate by her hair behind him. "I see you brought more meat to feast upon!"

One of the skeletal hands grabs my front leg, pulling me hard to the ground. I tumble, crushing several other arms that sprout up. We roll to our feet, roaring toward the demon.

"Stop." The words sear into my mind, my entire body freezing in place.

The demon frowns down at us, its nose bunched up to its brow. "How disgusting you animals are. Your weak, pathetic, little minds. To think my brothers and sisters fell to your kind," it hisses, spitting a black, oily substance on me. "What do you think my dear?" it asks, pulling Vera up by her hair.

"Just die," she grunts through gritted teeth.

A fire rages within me, battling to move even one inch. *Kill it! It's right there!*

The demon chuckles to himself, "You want him to just die?" His grin widening to its ears, "I agree."

Its pitch-black eyes look down at me as it twists its razor-sharp talons, thrusting them toward me.

"Just die," I grunt through gritted teeth. My world fades to whites and grays as the demon slows to a snail's pace.

A plume of black smoke flashes behind Amarak, the Seer's red and yellow eyes opening within it. "Debt," it whispers. Emerging from the shadows. Its razorlike talons reach for me, "Paid." With a tap the collar disintegrates to ash around my neck. Another flash of darkness and the Seer is gone.

The world returns to color, the demon chuckling to himself. "You want him to just die? I agree," it says, thrusting its talons toward Amarak.

My eyes pierce through his barriers as I grip his mind in my hand, freezing him in place.

"What?" it shrieks, its eyes darting about as it attempts to look at me.

Thousands of voices whisper through his mind. All crying out for vengeance. "How very interesting," I say, gasping for air.

"Wait, no, listen. I can help you. I know what Ogroz is planning."

I lean forward, whispering the words it spoke to me right before my entire life changed, "Would you like to see what you're capable of?" I force it to twist its claws towards its own chest.

"Wait! Stop! This isn't happening!"

"Let me show you," I growl, feeling the blood ooze over its talons as I force it to rip its own heart out. I feel the demon's agony washing over me as its last moments pass, staring at its own heart in its palm before collapsing to the ground in a pool of steaming black tar.

His mindscape vanishes with his last breath. I return to the world around me as Amarak nuzzles his head against my hand.

"I love you too," I say across our bond. Feeling every ounce of his happiness at the words. My eyes rise, taking in the carnage before us. Dozens of wolves approaching us as one. Their eyes shimmering with life. *"Your wolves are strong."*

"Our wolves," Alex says across the bond.

"Our family."

ABOUT THE AUTHOR

Joey Kincaid loves to read and write first person romance novels set in dark worlds. His favorite stories have devoted characters that would do anything for the ones they love.

Joey lives in Oregon with his wife, daughter, three young boys and a handful of fur babies. When he isn't enjoying time with his family he is probably reading, writing or playing video games.